D1442974

The Jig Is Up

Rachael O. Phillips

AnniesFiction.com

Books in the Scottish Bakehouse Mysteries series

. . . and more to come!

Library of Congress-in-Publication Data
The Jig Is Up / by Rachael O. Phillips
p. cm.
I. Title
            2019948989

AnniesFiction.com
(800) 282-6643
Scottish Bakehouse Mysteries™
Series Creator: Shari Lohner
Series Editor: Elizabeth Morrissey
Cover Illustrator: Bonnie Leick

10 11 12 13 14 | Printed in South Korea | 9 8 7 6 5 4 3

1

"Back in college, I never would've guessed that we'd open a bakery together someday," Molly Ferris said, clasping her two dearest friends' arms as they waited for their real estate agent.

Amid the group embrace, tall Carol MacCallan's mouth quirked in a wry grin. "We certainly never dreamed of buying an old funeral home together."

"We wouldn't be considering it now if Fergus hadn't told you about it." Laura Donovan cast a mischievous glance at Molly.

Fergus MacGregor, Molly's crush from long ago, would join them later. "It was nice of him to help us." Molly ignored the tendrils of warmth winding into her cheeks.

Carol rescued her. "Yes, wasn't it? Especially since there aren't many commercial properties for sale in Loch Mallaig."

A popular tourist destination in Michigan's Upper Peninsula, Loch Mallaig was a quaint town founded by Scottish pioneers in 1825—and from the Scotland-themed businesses to the faint brogue many residents had inherited from previous generations, the village stayed true to its bonny roots.

Laura twirled a lock of her auburn hair as she surveyed the peeling paint on the Victorian mansion's wraparound porch. "Not the cheeriest atmosphere for a bakery. Maybe the inside is nicer."

"You know that no house in Michigan—especially in the UP—is cheery in March," Carol pointed out. Though they'd scattered since college, the former roommates all had grown up in the Wolverine State.

Molly tipped her head back to scrutinize the house's upper stories. "Those shutters don't add much," she admitted. "They must be at least fifty years old."

"What color would you call that, anyway?" Laura wrinkled her nose. "Slime-green?"

"Easily replaced," Carol put in, ever the voice of reason. "Not like siding and windows." She tugged on Laura's coat sleeve. "Let's check those out while we're waiting for Beverly. She said the Baileys recently replaced the windows, but I'd like to see them for myself."

Leave it to Carol to zero in on practicalities. Molly grinned as they carefully navigated slippery sidewalks and deceptively deep snowdrifts. During college thirty years ago, Carol had saved them from putting a deposit on a darling apartment with hostile plumbing.

They circled the big house and confirmed Beverly's assessment of the lower story. The creamy yellow siding could use a power wash or some touching up, but after a long winter or two, what house wouldn't?

Molly couldn't add numbers in her head like Carol, the retired math teacher, but anyone could see that after paying for all this, the Baileys had probably had to wait on painting the porch and shutters.

A "Yoo-hoo!" drew them back to the front door.

"Did I get the time wrong?" Lochside Realty agent Beverly Scott's apologetic smile gleamed against her smooth, dark skin.

"Not at all," Molly assured her. "We're just nosy—wanted to see a little on our own."

"Feel free to look as much as you want." A freezing gust of wind reminded them it was still winter, and Beverly shivered as she inserted the old-fashioned key into the heavy, wooden front door, which had an elegant stained glass panel installed in the top half. "Come in, come in. My husband, Ethan, built a fire this morning to take off the chill."

He certainly knows how to help his wife sell properties. Molly and the others gave cries of delight at the sight of the enormous stone fireplace in the spacious front room. Flames crackled a friendly greeting as the women warmed their hands.

Beverly gestured at the worn carpet. "Of course, this would have to be replaced—although Mrs. Bailey did say that the floors underneath are hardwood taken from local pine trees."

Molly pictured the gleam of hardwood accented with colorful rugs. Perfect for rustic yet trendy decor. She shouldn't show too much interest too fast, but as a former Chicago event planner, she couldn't help mentally arranging tables and chairs around the fireplace.

Laura, eyes alight, seemed to follow a similar vein, pointing to the opposite end of the room. "We could put display cases over there for breads, scones, cookies, and so on."

Laura had left her position as chef at the hip 29 North restaurant in New York City to join their business venture. Molly could picture cases full of the spectacular pastries and desserts her friend would create for their customers.

Carol, who had run her own cake business on the side for years, inquired, "Is there room for a big kitchen on the main floor?"

"There's a kitchen down this hallway." Beverly led the way. "It's larger than you'd expect in a funeral home. But then, families in this area tend to be close-knit. I'm sure sizable groups gathered here for coffee and snacks." She smiled. "We all *love* to eat."

"That's good." Molly blinked as they entered the room, where huge windows magnified the bleak March sunshine. "It's much bigger than I anticipated."

Carol measured the walls with her eyes. "We'd have to install more ovens and more sinks, but there appears to be room for them."

Laura flung open one door, then another. "These must have been storerooms. They're the perfect size for a walk-in fridge and freezer."

Had they been closets? Or workrooms where bodies were stored or prepared for burial?

Molly shook off such thoughts. So far, the place presented good possibilities for their Scottish bakehouse, its theme a nod to the village's heritage as well as to their shared ancestry. If she and her friends were going to make their dream come true here, they couldn't afford to get bogged down in irrelevant details.

But she saw similar doubts on her friends' faces after viewing the upstairs, which included an office, storage, and living space. The Baileys had inhabited the ample apartment with its outdated, cranberry-and-mauve decor for years.

When Beverly excused herself to answer a phone call, Carol asked in a low voice, "How did they ever live above caskets and—and—"

"Dead people?" Laura finished for her. "At least the Baileys never had problems with noisy neighbors."

Despite the joke, her laugh sounded nearly as uneasy as Carol's, and Molly remembered that back in college, both had balked at visiting haunted fraternity houses at Halloween. Even adventurous Laura had her limits.

Molly scanned the kitchenette, bedroom, den, and full bath again. She shrugged off her own small shiver as new ideas beckoned. Reject a promising property for silly non-reasons? No way.

"C'mon." She summoned her most persuasive smile. "We're bigger than all that. We're bakers. We're brave. We're *women*." Molly struck the fist-in-the-air pose they had caricatured during college.

Carol and Laura both smiled at the memory.

Beverly bustled back. She must have sensed their underlying nervousness because she hurried them through a minimalistic tour of the bare attic with its "infinite storage space," then outside again, near the garage, where they almost ran Fergus down.

Molly had spoken with him only on the phone, but even after thirty years—and with his addition of a dark beard peppered faintly with gray—she would have recognized Fergus anywhere. He had the same twinkling blue eyes and devastating smile that had captured her teenage heart.

"Molly Kirkpatrick." His grin widened. "You haven't changed a bit."

She hadn't heard her maiden name in ages. Molly chuckled, trying to ignore the Scottish jig her heart was performing. "You fib much better than you used to." Sensing the others' eyes on them, she gestured toward the house. "Thanks for telling us about the property."

"Glad to help." Fergus turned to Beverly. "Have they seen the LaSalle yet?"

"The what?" Laura's forehead crinkled.

"It's an old car they don't make anymore," Carol said, wearing an equally puzzled expression.

"Is this car part of the deal?" Molly asked in surprise.

Beverly gave a slight cough as she unlocked the garage's side door. "We usually don't include vehicles in a real estate package. But Hennie insisted anyone who liked the home would like the LaSalle."

"It's a 1939 classic," Fergus enthused. "I'll open the main door so you can see it."

If you're so hooked on this car, why don't you buy it? Molly could almost hear her friends' thoughts.

Nevertheless, they all shifted position. With boyish excitement, Fergus bounded ahead, reached inside, and pressed the wall-mounted opener.

The heavy wooden door creaked open to reveal . . .

A hearse.

"Isn't she gorgeous?" Fergus sounded as if he were introducing them to his girlfriend.

Molly pushed aside a hint of annoyance at his dreamy tone. "It's certainly, um, elegant." Even the dust couldn't hide the LaSalle's classy lines.

"It is lovely in its own way." Carol was using her polite-teacher voice, the one that had probably gotten through more than one conference with a difficult parent.

Laura didn't bother. "So's the cemetery, but we're not setting up a bakery there either." She crossed her arms. "I'm sorry, but this whole place creeps me out. A hearse? Seriously?"

Carol hesitated. "It is somewhat unsettling."

Molly's gaze swept the mansion as well, and her heart sank as she glimpsed Beverly's and Fergus's tight smiles. If she and her partners refused this property, how long before they could open their bakery?

This is the right place for us. Hearse and all. Molly knew it, the way she'd known the bakery venture was what she really wanted. What they all wanted.

But how could she help the others see it?

Fergus cleared his throat. "You'll need a delivery vehicle, won't you? The LaSalle has plenty of space. You could deliver to the whole town in one trip."

Laura rolled her eyes, but Molly grabbed his words and a flash of inspiration. "It's perfect. We can call the bakery 'Bread on Arrival.' We'll use the LaSalle for deliveries."

Her partners gaped at her as if she'd lost her mind.

"'Bread on Arrival'?" A small grin blossomed on Laura's face.

"Don't you get it?" Molly summoned her best smile. "Once we remodel the house, polish up this beauty, and put a bright-colored logo on its doors—a loaf of bread, cupcakes, or whatever—the funeral-home-turned-bakery aspect will promote our business like nothing else. Our bakehouse will be one of a kind. Perfect for local advertising, and fabulous online."

Laura's brown eyes sparkled. Even Carol uncrossed her arms. A few weeks earlier they'd tried to envision a way to jump-start their business without success. Now they had finally found a viable solution.

"I think you have something there, partner." Laura's smile grew as she turned to Carol. "How about you, other partner?"

Carol slowly nodded. "We'll need to talk about it more. Maybe over lunch. My stomach's starting to growl."

"Of course," Beverly interjected smoothly as she closed the garage. "May I suggest Neeps and Tatties across the street?"

"That restaurant wasn't there back in the days when my family spent summers here." For the moment, Molly was glad to shift the subject. "I know 'tatties' is the Scottish word for potatoes. But what are neeps?"

"Great question," Beverly laughed. "Since Fergus has a Scottish background, I'll let him answer."

"Sure." Fergus beamed at them. "In Scotland, neeps are a lot like rutabagas. My mom mashes and serves neeps and tatties side by side, especially at holidays, like my grandmothers did. The ones at the restaurant"—he gestured with his thumb—"are almost as good."

Mmm. Molly's freezing nose could almost smell steaming, buttery vegetables or savory soup, but another possibility had occurred to her, one she wanted to ponder before discussing it with the others. "I'd like to peek inside one more time before lunch." She glanced at Beverly, who nodded. "Mind if I meet you there?"

"Sure. I'll drink your cup of hot chocolate too," Laura joked.

Carol grinned. "Let's go."

Molly watched her friends amble toward the restaurant, tossing bright-eyed glances over their shoulders at her and Fergus. In her absence, she suspected they'd discuss matchmaking more than the property, but it couldn't be helped. She wanted to go over the house again, especially that apartment.

Fergus accompanied Beverly and Molly, which shouldn't have surprised her. After all, he was the one who had connected them to this property. Even as a teen, he had taken interest in all things historical—especially in Loch Mallaig.

As they approached the front porch again, Molly ignored its peeling state, choosing to picture its gingerbread trim glistening with fresh white paint, maybe with lush ferns hanging from its arches. They would set big pots of coral geraniums here and there, with tall topiaries flanking the front door. She mentally added a couple of porch swings with pillows in cheerful prints where customers could linger over coffee and Laura's to-die-for pastries.

Voilà! All traces of funeral home gloomies gone.

Ideas leaped and danced through Molly's mind as Beverly led them around the first story and up the venerable carved staircase, then unlocked the landing door again and showed them into the apartment. Though Molly again winced at the sight of mauve walls and outdated wallpaper featuring cows in a field, she applied a mental paintbrush. A soft blue throughout would bring a summery Lake Superior vibe into the apartment. She'd paint the cabinets in the tiny kitchen white to lose the dark, dated feel. Molly opened one of the few drawers.

"The kitchen is small, but it would make a great break room," Beverly suggested.

"I don't believe Molly's thinking of using it for the business."

Fergus's voice made Molly jump. She'd almost forgotten he was there. But that quirky, raised brow and the knowing glint in his eyes told her he'd read her mind, just as he often had decades before.

Realizing that they were both watching her for a response, Molly smiled at Beverly. "Fergus is right. Of course we'd need the office and storage room for the bakery. But if we buy the property, I might consider living here. After it's updated, of course."

Beverly blinked, but quickly listed the advantages. "Your walk to work will be the shortest in town. That would be especially nice in January."

Molly nodded. "I loved Chicago, but I hated commuting to work." Her mind was already listing larger pieces of furniture she could give her daughter, Chloe, who had just bought her first house.

Slow down, Molly ordered herself. She and her partners certainly couldn't buy the place with only one walk-through. Even if they did end up purchasing it, Carol and Laura would have to agree to her living in the apartment. "Right now, it's only a thought—something we'll discuss."

"Of course," Beverly said. "Do you want to revisit anything else in the house? If you'd like to do it on your own, I'll leave the key with you. You can drop it off at my office later."

"That would be great. Thanks for your help." As Molly took the key and shook hands with Beverly, her disobedient mind continued to race. *I'll keep the love seat, but the big sectional will have to go. Grandma Kirkpatrick's chairs probably will have to be reupholstered, but they're the perfect size for that den.*

Beverly started down the staircase but paused and called, "Don't worry about the fire downstairs. Ethan will drop by during his lunch hour and take care of it."

Moments later, the front door thumped shut.

Molly hadn't anticipated being alone with Fergus. She definitely didn't mean for her own glance to intercept his.

Easy, girl. "This place needs work, but it has possibilities." She moved across the room and examined the refrigerator and range. This was just a time to catch up with an old friend. A handsome old friend. "These seem reasonably new, and given the kitchen on the main floor, I don't need anything bigger. In fact, I don't want anything bigger."

Fergus nodded. "Traveling light these days, are you?"

Molly opened a cabinet and stared at its empty shelves. "Yes. I'm done with keeping up a full-size home alone. It's been more than a decade since my husband, Kevin, passed away."

"I'm sorry."

She knew he didn't say it lightly. "Thank you. But I've weathered that, and my daughter, Chloe, has left the nest. She's a veterinarian in Milwaukee."

"My son, Neil, lives just down the road from me. He's a big help in the business." Fergus owned the Castleglen resort and lodge, which his grandfather had started with just a golf course. "But I must say it was hard when my little girl, Blair, grew up on me. She lives in Indianapolis."

"Never easy, is it?" Molly knew Fergus and his ex-wife, Lucy, had divorced years before, but she wasn't about to mention it.

He laughed outright. "Oh, on some days, letting Blair go was the easiest thing I ever did. She is a redhead after all."

They wandered through the rooms again, chatting comfortably all the while—sometimes catching up, sometimes brainstorming remodeling possibilities. Fergus had learned a lot about renovations while running Castleglen, and he offered to help Molly and her partners in any way he could, whether they bought the funeral home or another property. Fergus also knew "the best handyman in the Upper Peninsula," Hamish Bruce.

"He's an eccentric old codger, but he knows his stuff," Fergus said. "When you've decided on a place, I'll introduce you."

Once they'd finished touring, Molly feared another awkward moment. Did Fergus expect an invitation to lunch? She and her partners really needed to talk. Alone.

Besides, too much time spent with him might complicate matters, and Molly wanted life to stay simple. At least for a while.

Fergus solved her dilemma neatly by saying he had a meeting with Neil to discuss business matters. Was it her imagination, or did his smile hold just the right amount of regret?

Molly waved as he headed to his Range Rover, with its abundant, polished chrome, parked along a side street. Obviously, he still liked sharp cars. *I'll bet it has leather upholstery.*

She bundled up, locked the front door, then gazed up at the big house one more time. Could she persuade her partners to buy this lovely old mansion that had already begun to seem like home?

As she followed the delicious noontime fragrances wafting from Neeps and Tatties, seasoned public relations warrior Molly prepared to give it her best shot.

2

A few weeks later, light from the chandeliers at King's Heid Pub glimmered in Molly's glass as she raised it high. "To Bread on Arrival! May it be the best Scottish bakehouse Michigan's Upper Peninsula has ever seen."

Laura, Carol, her husband, Harvey, and Fergus echoed her elation and drank the toast, but Fergus, who owned the restaurant, raised his glass a second time.

"To three lovely ladies who will improve our community with their sweet presence." He patted his stomach. "And their sweet treats. I can hardly wait."

Laura toasted him in return. "I'll make you a chocolate truffle cake so rich, even you will gain weight."

Laughing, they clinked glasses. Gratitude surged through Molly as she drank. Not only had Fergus helped them find the funeral home, but he had already committed to standing orders of their bread and pastries for his two restaurants. When Molly and her friends had closed on their new property, they had unanimously voted King's Heid as the perfect place to celebrate.

"Fergus, we can't thank you enough for your help." Molly allowed extra warmth to seep into her words.

"It was my pleasure." His gaze rested on her a moment, then shifted to the red-haired man approaching their table. "Allow me to introduce my son, Neil. He's the brains of my business."

"Oh, sure, Dad. Georgetown taught me everything I need to know, and I didn't learn a *thing* from you," the tall, young man joked. Shaking hands, Neil flashed a smile that rivaled his father's. He exchanged a few pleasantries, then excused himself to make rounds of the kitchen and serving areas. Molly couldn't imagine Neil would find any flaws. The maple-glazed Chinook salmon—caught that day in Lake Superior, according to their waiter—had tasted heavenly. The dining room, with its rich wall tapestries, polished antique weapon displays, and spotless white tablecloths, extended a royal welcome to the guests. Molly was pleased to note that the place was packed, despite it being the off-season.

"Neil's on the quiet side—always has been—but he does a great job with the staff." Fergus's voice rang with pride in his son. "So glad my kids are smarter than me."

"Oh, right." Molly rolled her eyes. "Don't be silly, Fergus. We know he's learning from the best. We'll take lessons too."

"Any lessons you want to teach us," Carol said. "We have a lot to learn—and a lot to do—between now and our grand opening." She consulted her phone's calendar. "Goodness, March is nearly over. Still, I think we'll be ready by the end of April."

"We can do it." Laura clasped her partners' hands. "I can hardly wait to get started." Little by little, she'd reversed her stance on the funeral home. Now her enthusiasm leavened her partners' like yeast in her brioche.

"Watch out," Harvey teased, shooting a warning glance at Fergus. "These three have always been dangerous together."

"You've got that right." Carol winked at her husband, and he clutched his heart.

Fergus joined Harvey in a fake show of fear. "Och no!"

"Och yes." Molly raised her chin in mock defiance. "As Dad used to say, 'The three Scottish hens are on the loose again.'" She grinned wickedly at the phrase. "Loch Mallaig will never be the same."

By the end of the following morning, Molly wondered if her *back* would ever be the same. Though she, Carol, and Laura had each claimed a section of the large main room, taping it in preparation for painting was taking forever. The tall windows, ornate woodwork, and built-in cabinets with beautiful lead glass required extra care.

Stop whining, Molly admonished her creaking bones as she carried in buckets of paint and other supplies. Had she thought a dream come true would happen by magic?

"Whose idea was this, anyway?" Carol demanded from the top of a ladder, where she was taping off crown molding.

"Let's blame Molly." Hunkered next to the baseboard, Laura peered up at her, a mischievous light in her eyes. "In fact, we should let Molly do it all, since she's going to live here."

Setting the paint buckets on the floor with a thud, Molly sugared her voice. "Oh, you can live here too. We could all share that apartment, just like we did in college. So what if there's only one bedroom? We could do bunk beds."

Laura snorted. "We're good friends, but not *that* good. I'm glad I've got the lease on my rental cottage signed."

"I don't think Harvey would like that arrangement," Carol commented. "He's already in love with our new log home, and I'm pretty sure he likes having me there too. And both of you, of course." Molly and Laura were staying with the MacCallans until they moved into their own places.

"Oh, I'm sure Harvey thanks his lucky stars every night that he's got two extra roommates," Laura said with a chuckle. "A retirement dream come true."

Molly luxuriated in banter and laughter as they worked. It was so good to be with friends again. And she was so happy that at day's end, sad goodbyes and long distances no longer separated them.

Halfway through the morning, though, Carol asked Molly how Chloe had reacted to their purchase.

Molly gulped, mentally scrambling for an answer.

"You haven't told her?" Carol lowered her chin, nailing Molly with the sharp expression that had cowed many an unruly student.

"She doesn't need to know everything that goes on in my life," Molly retorted.

Laura added a "you've got to be kidding" stare to Carol's.

"Okay, I just sounded like your average seventeen-year-old," Molly admitted, then sighed. "Chloe liked the job opportunity in Milwaukee better than two other possibilities farther south. It pays more too. But she also wanted to live somewhere where we could visit on a regular basis. Now we're more than six hours apart, rather than just the two-hour train ride that separates Milwaukee and Chicago."

"I get that." Carol patted her shoulder. "Harvey and I are lucky." The fact their daughter and her family lived in Loch Mallaig had made their move from Pennsylvania an easy decision.

"Still, it's not like you moved to Alaska." Laura rolled her eyes. "You didn't promise her you'd stay in Chicago forever, did you?"

"Well, no. But children are like that, regardless of age." How could Molly explain this to Laura? Happily single, she didn't under-stand—though she should. Laura now lived only two hours away from her family, the proximity to her aging parents being part of the reason she'd made the move. Molly shrugged. "Kids assume parents will always be available."

"But you have your own life to live too," Laura insisted.

"And we're so glad you want to share it with us." Carol, who did understand, squeezed Molly's hand. "But Chloe deserves to know, just as you should know about her major life decisions, don't you think?"

Molly groaned. "Do you two always have to be right?"

"No. Just ninety-nine percent of the time," Carol declared with a smirk.

"So call Chloe." Laura pulled Molly's phone from her jeans pocket and dangled it in her face. "Now, before you talk yourself out of it."

Molly grabbed the phone. "I'll call her tonight."

"No you won't." Carol eyed her. "Didn't you say Chloe works from noon into the evening most Mondays?"

Molly frowned. "Not only are you two bossy, your memories are too good."

"So call her." Laura's teasing tone faded to serious. "The longer you delay, the madder she'll be."

True. "All right, all right. I'll call—but you girls get back to work. No eavesdropping." Her face grim, Molly headed for the kitchen.

She took a deep breath and another, then hit speed dial. Too late, Molly wondered if she'd awaken her sleep-loving daughter.

"Hey, Mom." Chloe sounded almost cheery, relieving the smallest of Molly's concerns.

"Hi, sweetie. How are you?"

They exchanged chitchat about Chloe's new house and a scary but successful surgery she'd performed on a family's beloved Irish setter, but the younger Ferris woman soon cut to the chase. "So have you seen any property that might work for your bakery-in-the-wild?"

Molly swallowed. "As a matter of fact, I—I mean, we, Carol and Laura and I—bought a building."

"You already bought it?" Chloe's voice went up an octave. "I thought you were just looking."

Molly knew she'd given Chloe that impression, and shame washed over her. "This place was an excellent deal. We figured we'd better snap it up before someone else bought it." Molly tried to ignore how many months the funeral parlor had remained empty.

Chloe pounced on the fib. "Yes, we all know that thousands of businesses are competing for space in northern Michigan. With the bears."

"I haven't seen a single bear." *Even though they do prowl around the edge of town sometimes.*

Her daughter sniffed. "Yet."

Hoping to get the conversation back on track, Molly focused on the positive. "Seriously, it's beautiful here—lake, evergreens, quaint little town. The house is a big old Victorian with gingerbread trim and a gorgeous wraparound porch. It just needs a little work."

"I'll bet." Despite her skepticism, a note of curiosity crept into Chloe's voice. "So you're remodeling a big old house?"

"Ah, yes." This time, it was Molly's voice that went up an octave.

"Mom, what aren't you telling me?"

Giving up, Molly plunged in. "It's an old funeral parlor."

"A *what?*"

"It was a mortuary," Molly said, then added brightly, "We're going to use its history as a PR tool."

"How could you possibly sell baked goods using a funeral theme?" Chloe practically shrieked the words.

"We're calling it Bread on Arrival. We bought the hearse too."

"The *hearse?*"

"We'll use it as a delivery vehicle."

Chloe remained silent for so long that Molly thought she'd hung up.

"Hello?" Molly ventured softly. "Are you still there?"

"I'm here." Her daughter took a deep breath. "Couldn't your midlife crisis just be buying a motorcycle like a normal person?"

Returning to the main room, Molly stuffed her phone into her pocket like a pistol into a holster.

Carol took one look at her and grimaced. "Chloe didn't handle it very well, did she?"

"You could say that." Her daughter's forced courtesy during the remainder of the phone call had reminded Molly of ice on a puddle—brittle, with plenty of mud underneath.

"Give her time," Laura urged. "She'll get used to the idea."

"Maybe." *In a year. Or five.* Nevertheless, Molly straightened her shoulders and returned to her task. "At least she knows now. I don't have to keep rehearsing speeches."

Strangely, taping woodwork no longer felt like drudgery. Compared to dealing with a disgruntled adult daughter, it seemed uncomplicated, even easy. Molly threw herself into her work, as did Carol and Laura, all eager to forget about the phone call.

Fergus surprised them by appearing at eleven o'clock, though he'd said he wouldn't be free to help until the afternoon. A tall, wiry, white-bearded man accompanied him. His eyes reminded Molly of a hawk's as he scrutinized each of the three women.

Fergus introduced him. "This is Hamish Bruce, my former history teacher. Now he's the best handyman in the UP."

"An exaggeration, lad," Hamish admonished Fergus as if he were a teenager instead of a man in his early fifties. "But only a little."

He sounded serious. Molly exchanged glances with her partners while Hamish paced the room, inspecting it as if he were in charge of the entire project. They needed help, but what was Fergus getting them into?

"I used to help out the Baileys sometimes," the old man continued in his faint Scottish brogue, "so I know there's a kitchen here—one that'll need changes if you're going to open a bakery." He started down the hall. "I like to do kitchens."

"Hamish remodeled mine at King's Heid," Fergus explained as they trailed after the older man, who seemed to have already hired himself. "He saved me all kinds of money, and my chef is still raving."

Thank goodness. Molly sensed the others' relief too.

Upon entering the kitchen, Hamish whipped out a tape measure. "Probably need a commercial oven—"

"Two commercial ovens," Carol interjected. "We hope to do lots of wedding cakes, along with breads and pastries."

"More sinks for cleanup too," Laura added.

"My department, probably," Molly said as Hamish began measuring and muttering to himself.

"You bake, don't you?" Fergus asked. "I recall eating incredible blackberry pie at your summer cottage."

He'd remembered her specialty. Molly brushed off her pleasure. "I do pies and basic cakes and breads. I'll help out. But Laura and Carol are the real bakers in this business. I'm the marketing person, the counter lady, the cleanup guru, and whatever else we need."

"You get to drive that hearse." Laura hadn't quite reconciled with the LaSalle.

"I'd love to. But it has a manual transmission." Molly pictured the vintage car jolting and jerking through downtown as she mishandled the gear shift. No wedding cake would survive that.

"No problem there." Fergus's face lit up, and Molly's stomach fluttered. "I'll teach you."

Calm down, Molly. He just wants to drive that car. "Thanks." Molly smiled. "I might take you up on that after we get this place going."

Hamish moved faster than Molly would have expected from a man his age. Examining the proposed walk-in refrigerator and freezer space, he said, "Ah, the embalming areas. Didn't work around there much." He scratched his neatly trimmed beard. "Jim Bailey was a good man with a noble occupation. Not easy, you know, preparing folks for their heavenly homes. Och, some were ugly as a bucket of frogs when they came in. Took a real trick or two to make them pretty in a casket."

Laura and Carol froze. Molly thanked heaven they'd already signed the mortgage contract.

Her partners' reaction didn't register on Hamish's radar. "Jim took care of all my family." He puffed out his chest. "My great-great-grandfather helped found this town. We're pure Scots, of course, related to Robert the Bruce."

Any subject was better than embalming, so Molly pounced. "The Scottish hero?"

A big smile—his first—filled Hamish's face. "None other." Continuing his inspection, he spouted a treatise on Bruce's exploits but eventually wandered back to what he considered the subject at hand. "Jim Bailey and his kin always took care of the founding families. Even did the mayor a couple of years ago. Mayor Kinnaird, I mean. Not Mayor Calhoun, who's in office now."

When Laura interrupted Hamish with appliance alternatives she'd researched, the man's heavy, white brows scrunched over his eyes.

Sorry, Hamish. It's our project, not yours. Over the years, Molly had encountered other experts who tried to take over. They'd always thought they knew what she needed better than she did.

Carol leaped into the discussion. As she and Laura revealed their plans for the kitchen, Hamish's brows relaxed, and he eventually gave a grudging nod of approval and agreed to do what they wanted. "I see these hens know their work," he told Fergus as he headed upstairs without invitation.

Molly halted on the first step. Laura's brown eyes snapped. Carol's expression said she wanted to give Hamish detention.

Fergus risked a glance backward, then hastily followed the handyman upstairs.

Of course the "hens" knew the expression was a common Scottish term for "women," one that even Molly's father used. But coming from Hamish, it sounded decidedly uncomplimentary. Molly paused, seeing her own debate mirrored in her partners' taut faces. Could they tolerate the outspoken man for a few weeks in order to get the bakehouse going? Or should they show "the best handyman in the UP" the door and lock it behind him?

Molly took a deep breath. "I'm going to see what he has to say about the upstairs."

"Have fun," Laura muttered.

"Good luck." Carol cast a sympathetic glance at Molly, then started back toward the main room with Laura.

"No, no," Molly protested, "I need your help. Safety in numbers, you know. Besides, working with Hamish has to be a joint decision. We should do this together."

The other women sighed and followed Molly to the apartment, probably to watch the fireworks that would ensue. Molly sighed too, but she'd handled difficult people before. She could do this. To make her dream come true, she *would* do this—for a limited time.

Her smile seemed to startle Fergus. Hamish didn't appear to notice, of course. But Molly needed all her tools of persuasion, and a smile always warmed her voice. She honeyed her next words. "My, you work quickly, Hamish."

He was going over the kitchenette. "No sense in wasting my time and yours."

"I agree. We're not wasting money either. Other than painting it and adding a backsplash, I'm leaving this kitchen as is. So let's move on to the business rooms. For starters, we'd like a new exterior door in the office. And we'll need shelving in the storeroom."

Hamish seemed to soften a little as Molly explained their plans for the upper story. *Maybe he just needs a firm hand.*

Finally, she, Carol, and Laura found themselves agreeing to Hamish's reasonable hourly charge. The next day, he began painting, installing, and constructing at lightning speed—and doing it well.

As the main story's new appearance took shape, Molly mused at the gift Fergus had sent their way.

If only Hamish and his monologue had an "off" button.

Even when the prospect of opening the bakehouse in Loch Mallaig had been little more than a dream for the three women, Carol and Harvey had moved to town to be closer to their daughter, Jenny, and her family. The MacCallans were well established in their large log house, so Laura and Molly felt like they were returning to a real home at the end of each long, hard day. The only thing missing for Molly was her Scottish terrier, Angus.

Not wanting to impose or traumatize the MacCallans' cat, Pascal, Molly had insisted on boarding Angus at a kennel in Copper Harbor. Now, though, she missed her beloved Scottie so much that she secretly wished she'd taken the couple up on their invitation to let Angus stay with them.

For months, Molly had pictured the trio's first weeks together in Loch Mallaig. Every night, they'd sit in front of the MacCallans' fireplace and sip herbal tea or indulge in big mugs of hot chocolate topped with mountains of whipped cream. Their wee-hour gabfests would drive Harvey to ice fishing.

Instead, after working at the bakehouse all day, the reunited roommates microwaved frozen dinners, then fell into bed. Molly hadn't slept so well in years.

Despite better rest, she didn't welcome a nudge one morning before the alarm went off.

"Molly. Wake up."

Her foggy brain cells, occupied with a dream that combined Laura's chocolate éclairs and an international hearse race, ignored the hand poking her shoulder.

When it refused to cease and desist, Molly turned over. "Go away. Too early to paint."

"It's not really," Carol's no-nonsense voice intoned, "but that isn't why I'm dragging you out. The police called. Somebody broke into our bakehouse."

3

Molly bolted upright in bed. Her friend's guest room, with its classic lodge decor, swung into focus. "Did I hear you right?"

"You did." Carol handed her a to-go cup of coffee. "Laura's getting dressed. An officer is meeting us there in twenty minutes."

Molly wanted to ask a dozen questions, but the sooner they arrived at the bakery, the sooner they'd learn the details. She grimaced as she threw on jeans and a sweatshirt. Living in Chicago had numbed her to "minor" crimes like a break-in, but how could that happen in quaint little Loch Mallaig? She tried to ward off a shiver with a sip of coffee, but the hot liquid did little to warm her.

However, by the time they arrived at the bakehouse—before the police officer—Molly's temper had heated her through and through. And as they slowly picked their way along the snowy sidewalk, the chill didn't cool her one bit.

Laura, gripping her own coffee like a buoy, also steamed hotter than her drink. "Well, hello, New York City. I thought I'd left you behind."

Carol tried to reassure them—and herself?—that Jenny and her husband, Craig, considered Loch Mallaig a perfectly safe place to raise their children. "Still, I guess it isn't Disney World. My guess is that some kid had too much time on his hands and got creative."

A blood-red, spray-painted message on the siding near the back door appeared to confirm her hypothesis.

Trolls go home.

Trolls? In addition to many other meanings, it was locally a not-so-friendly term for Michiganders living south of the Mackinac Bridge that connected the state's lower and upper peninsulas.

Molly felt her friends' flinches almost as strongly as her own.

"So this is Loch Mallaig's idea of a welcome wagon?" Laura's eyes had narrowed to slits.

Molly tried to stay objective. "We'd better keep away from the porch," she cautioned. "Maybe the police still want to check for footprints or fingerprints."

"I wish everybody thought of that." A tall, fiftyish policeman approaching their group extended his hand. "I'm Broderick Gillespie, the department's deputy chief."

"I wish we were meeting under different circumstances," Laura said wryly, then shook his offered hand. "Laura Donovan."

After introductions from Carol and Molly, Deputy Chief Gillespie gestured toward the porch. "I examined the scene earlier, so remaining out in the cold won't be necessary. I didn't see evidence that the intruder actually entered. Still, I'd like you to double-check whether anything inside is missing or damaged."

"We'll try to help." Molly exchanged glances with the others, then followed him to the door. "We only closed on the bakery a short time ago."

"So I hear." The black-haired policeman, who appeared to be at least partially of Native American descent, shook his head. "I'm sorry this happened. Believe it or not, most people here appreciate new businesses, especially if they don't compete with established ones."

Molly nodded. "We researched all that during the early stages, making sure there were no other bakeries in the area."

Gillespie led the way up the steps to the back entrance. He pointed to a hand-size hole in one of the door's glass panes. "The perp cut and removed the glass, then reached through and turned the dead bolt. I'd replace this door with a solid one, if I were you."

"Absolutely." Laura glared at the door as if the burglary were its fault.

"But you said you didn't see evidence that this person went inside," Carol said. "If he or she went to all this trouble, why not?"

"I'm guessing the intruder heard something—maybe Officer Drummond, who called this in—and ran off before he could cause real trouble. I did find new boot prints in the snow that took off toward the side yard, then stopped at a plowed parking lot." Gillespie indicated the direction with his thumb. "There's no spray paint inside. Lots of fingerprints and footprints, but nothing fresh I could see. They could belong to you ladies, other prospective buyers, the Baileys, or even folks who attended funerals here. This place has been sitting empty for a long time, so who knows?" He shook his head. "Let's do a walk-through to see if anything was stolen."

In the dreary, early morning light, the blackened logs in the fireplace emphasized the main room's bleakness. The small areas the partners had spackled but not yet painted added nothing cheery.

They hadn't moved all their boxes to the bakery from storage yet, but the dozen they'd brought appeared intact.

Carol nosed around stacks with a small flashlight she'd brought. "I don't think they've been opened."

"I don't see any missing tools," Laura said, her voice dejected, and Molly and Carol both grunted out agreements.

"But we've mostly just scraped, spackled, and painted." Carol frowned. "Hamish will have to check whether the guy took any of his equipment."

What a monologue *that* would generate. Molly didn't want to imagine what Hamish would say if a thief had so much as touched a hair on his paintbrushes.

Laura's and Carol's expressions mirrored her thoughts. Maybe they could be gone when Hamish took his tour with the deputy chief.

When they'd finished looking around, the policeman thanked them for their cooperation.

On the way out the door, Molly glanced once more at the hole in the door's window, then at the surrounding floors of the hallway and outside porch. She turned to Gillespie. "I don't see any shattered glass. Did you take it to check for fingerprints?"

"I took it, but it wasn't shattered. Actually, I found a couple of big pieces in there." He pointed at a large, black trash receptacle beside the back stoop. "No fingerprints, but they fit the hole exactly."

The glass might have fit the hole, but in Molly's mind, something else didn't fit at all.

Later, as they sat around the MacCallans' kitchen table and devoured the comforting waffles Harvey had made, Molly voiced her thoughts about their prowler. "I agree with Deputy Chief Gillespie. Something scared the intruder off before he could vandalize inside or steal. But Carol, do you think he was a teen? Would a bored kid cut glass that carefully, then, just as carefully, dispose of it in a trash can?"

Carol shook her head. "The spray paint seemed to indicate our burglar was young, but if one of my high school students broke in, he'd smash the glass with a rock or hammer or even his fist." She sniffed. "He sure wouldn't clean up afterward."

Laura stabbed at her waffle. "From what Beverly and the officer said, our bakehouse has been empty for months. Has anybody else tried to break in? If not, why now?"

Molly tried to think of some other reason for the nasty message. "Maybe the burglar was looking for something specific. Would Hennie Bailey have any idea what it was?"

The former owner—a widowed Las Vegas native with a big, blonde hairdo who now kept mostly to herself in a small house on the outskirts of town—had been cordial but restrained throughout their business negotiations.

Laura put down her fork. "What if she has something to hide?"

"You three think too much," Harvey said from the counter as he carefully removed another perfectly golden waffle from the iron.

"You're right, honey." Carol paused in her task of bringing more juice to the table and gave him a peck on the cheek. "We ought to be savoring your waffles."

"Less talking, more chewing." Molly smiled at Harvey as he flipped the fresh waffle onto her plate, then she poured warm maple syrup over it and hummed appreciatively as she took a bite.

Molly pinned her question about Hennie to her mind's bulletin board, then joined in as they all tried to steer breakfast chitchat toward decorating the bakehouse. Despite the conversation's forced optimism, however, she knew that the intruder, whoever he was, had left his ghost to whisper uneasy questions in their ears.

"Och, what sort of news is this? Some dirty hooligan has broken into the house?"

Molly winced as Hamish glared at Deputy Chief Gillespie and continued his tirade. *It's not Gillespie's fault,* she wanted to say. *And, it's not like this is* your *building.*

From their expressions, Laura and Carol also wished they'd missed this little drama. But the deputy chief had wanted to talk to Hamish as soon as possible.

Despite the handyman's rant, Gillespie didn't bat an eyelash. He calmly steered Hamish through checking his toolbox and work areas. When Hamish discovered nothing missing, the loud rant quieted to occasional mutterings.

Gillespie thanked him for his help and promised to continue following the case closely.

"See that you do. We can't have criminals running loose around town." Hamish dismissed the officer and dug into his morning tasks with even more energy than usual.

As Molly saw Gillespie to the door, she grabbed the opportunity to ask the question she'd shelved. "Is it possible that something in the funeral parlor's history might have precipitated the break-in?"

"I spoke with Hennie Bailey a little while ago," Gillespie said. "She's as surprised as anyone. Some funeral home directors encounter vandalism, especially at Halloween. But she and Jim never had trouble like that, not in all the years they ran the place."

After the policeman was gone, Molly recounted the information to her friends.

"We're just lucky I guess," Laura groused.

"We can be thankful the burglar didn't have a chance to do much." Carol straightened her spine. "I found an old paint can labeled 'exterior siding' in the basement. Let's get a match mixed up today so we can cover that spray paint."

"All right," Laura said, only somewhat begrudgingly.

"Great idea, Carol," Molly agreed, glad that their steadfast friend had suggested an action that would help them move forward. Did that burglar, whoever he was, think these Scottish hens would flap and squawk and run away?

Abandon our dream? Molly bristled. *You have no idea who you're dealing with.*

But he'd soon find out.

Someone was knocking at the bakehouse's front door. Again. Molly's sore muscles complained as she straightened, but she didn't mind taking a break from painting around the fireplace.

Who could it be this time? The previous day, a German lady named Helga—perhaps the only non-Scot in town—had welcomed them with note cards from her nearby shop, The Pied Paper. The owner of the town drugstore had also dropped by. What was his name? Mac-something? Molly couldn't remember.

Both pleasant visitors had expressed delight at Bread on Arrival's opening in Loch Mallaig. Neither had mentioned their bakehouse's vandalism and near-burglary, so Molly and Laura had wondered if the incident had escaped the grasp of the local newspaper, the *Crown Press News*.

Carol had disagreed. "Jenny told me news travels around this town faster than any social media," she had argued. "Newspaper or not, Helga's heard something. I've visited her shop only once or twice, but those big brown eyes were casing our place as if *she* planned to break in."

This morning, the sight of Joyce Bruce, Hamish's wife, on the doorstep brightened Molly's mood. The smiling, gray-haired woman opened a big picnic basket to reveal gigantic muffins and a large thermos of coffee.

"I almost didn't bring the muffins," Joyce confessed. "Me, give muffins to bakers? What was I thinking?" Her twinkling brown eyes scanned Molly's tired face. "But I thought chocolate espresso muffins might give you all a boost."

"Bless you. I'll take caffeine in any form. Especially when it smells so delicious." Hugging the short, sweet lady seemed natural, though Molly had known her only a few days. "Should we call Hamish to join us?"

"Hamish already devoured his. He wanted to get back to work," Joyce explained as she stepped inside.

That didn't surprise Molly. The man never seemed to run down, even when doing a job as tiring as scraping paint off the porch's gingerbread trim.

"Coffee break!" Molly called toward the kitchen. "Joyce brought goodies."

Laura and Carol, both splattered with light-gray paint, hurried to join them, clearly not minding the interruption either.

As they enjoyed the refreshments, Joyce cooed appreciatively over the progress they'd made in the main room.

"Hamish's painting the ceiling sped up the process," Carol said, and the others nodded.

"We thought we knew how much work this would be." Laura laughed. "We had no idea what we were getting ourselves into. We never could have accomplished this much without him."

"I'm glad Hamish is able to help you girls." Joyce shot them a sideways grin. "It's also kept him busy."

And out of your hair. Molly read the same thought in her partners' faces, along with admiration for Joyce. They'd put up with his quirks for only a week. She'd been married to Hamish for forty-three years.

Joyce admired the new color on the walls. "That cream color will go with anything, and it really lightens this room's atmosphere. Accents the woodwork and fireplace too."

Laura nodded eagerly. "The color will make a great backdrop for those antique display cases you helped us find."

Joyce beamed. She had connected them with the owner of a

long-standing antiques shop in a neighboring town. The man was retiring, so they'd procured not only several beautiful cases but vintage sconces as well.

Carol beckoned. "Come see the kitchen."

Almost-completed gray walls contrasted with white windowsills and cabinets, creating a crisp, clean effect. Shining stainless steel work areas and sinks added to the trendy yet efficient aesthetic. The glass tile backsplash hadn't yet been installed, but Hamish had put in stylish new lighting fixtures the evening before.

"Gorgeous. Even Hamish might want to cook in this kitchen." Joyce's laughter said otherwise.

Another rap sounded on the front door, and Molly hurried to answer it. This time, a thirtyish woman and man, both with the red hair that was ubiquitous in Loch Mallaig, stood on the porch.

"Hello," Molly greeted the visitors. Before she could say anything else, Carol stepped forward and addressed the woman.

"You're Doreen Giobsan, aren't you? The owner of Thistle and That next door?" When the woman nodded, Carol continued, "My daughter, Jenny Gilmore, loves your gift shop, but I haven't had a chance to check it out."

"I can see why. Wow! You've been busy." Doreen's inquisitive gaze ran over the room. She gestured toward her companion. "For the record, this is *not* my husband. We're friends. And just barely."

The athletically built man chuckled and introduced himself as Dallis Witherspoon, a fitness instructor. "Doreen and I got nosy at the same time, I guess. Ran into her on the sidewalk."

"Hey, we're not as nosy as *some* people," Doreen said, nudging Joyce with an elbow.

"You're right. I'm shameless." Joyce chuckled. "At least I bring food."

"And you brought enough for everyone," Laura said.

Dallis poured himself a cup of coffee and Doreen snacked on a muffin as Molly and company conducted another lower-story tour. They laughed and chatted with their new friends, who gasped at the funeral home's transformation. Returning to the front room, they encountered Hamish.

He stared at them as if they were truant sixth graders.

The conversation crashed.

Doreen suddenly remembered that she *had* to get back to her shop. As she left, Dallis addressed his tour guides. "Thanks for showing us around, but I have an appointment in fifteen minutes. I'll let you all get back to work." His smile returned, and a note of persuasion colored his voice. "Before I leave, though, I should tell you the whole reason I stopped by. I lead the town's Scottish dance group, the Leaping Lowlanders. We'd love to have you join us."

No you wouldn't. Molly smothered a grin. "Thanks. We love all things Scottish, but I don't know a jig from a Highland fling. And coordination isn't my strong point."

"We'd be glad to teach you," Dallis said.

"Sure, if I can learn sitting down." Molly swept a hand around the room. "Right now, this project takes all my energy, plus some."

"Amen to that," Carol agreed, and Laura nodded.

"Weel, maybe you should all rest some mor-r-re." Apparently, Hamish's mild Scottish burr increased with sarcasm. As he marched into the kitchen. Joyce closed her eyes and shook her head.

Poor woman. Molly and the others glared after him. Did Hamish gripe when she dared drink half a cup of tea?

But Molly's concern soon morphed into glee when Joyce marched after him with a glint in her eye.

"Boy, is Hamish in for it," Laura stage whispered.

Carol pantomimed applause, and Molly joined in.

Hamish might consider himself their teacher, but his wife was definitely the principal.

Another bucket of paint. As she stirred it, Molly glared at the project they'd forgotten. How had these dingy kitchen cabinet interiors escaped their notice? They should have been done before the walls.

She'd expected Hamish to scold them, but Joyce's lecture had made a significant difference in his attitude. With only a small humph, he'd gone upstairs to work on the office.

Molly's partners regarded the leftover task without enthusiasm, but Carol brought her paint pan to fill and grabbed a small brush.

Laura, waiting her turn, clasped her hands and stretched. "I'm glad we decided to hire refinishers to do the floors. I'm not twenty-five anymore."

Molly agreed. "Ripping up the carpet and hauling it out wasn't exactly fun, but think how gorgeous the floors will be when they're done. Now we only have to do these cabinets and we will have finished the entire main floor. In record time, I'll bet."

Her friends' eyes brightened. Carol threw open a cabinet, reached in, and ran a dustcloth over its top shelf. "From the outside, nobody would ever guess these cabinets are this deep." She paused. "What's this?" She pulled out a smudged, somewhat wrinkled envelope, and examined it. "No address."

"Maybe a bill somebody forgot to pay?" Laura poured paint into her pan.

Carol frowned. "I think it's a letter."

Molly replaced the lid on the paint can, then examined the envelope Carol held. "There's no address," she noticed. "Perhaps we should take a look at it."

They all gathered around as Carol unfolded the plain, off-white sheet with a few sentences typewritten on it. "No date. This doesn't seem to be super old, but I imagine it's been a while since it was typed." Molly read aloud. "'To Whom It May Concern.'"

"That narrows it down," Carol joked.

Their smiles quickly vanished as they read the rest of the letter.

The coroner said Douglas Kinnaird's death was due to natural causes. But a closer examination of the facts will show there was nothing natural about it.

Douglas was murdered.

Molly swallowed hard.

"What in the world?" Laura whispered.

Carol said nothing. Her expression indicated she was as thunderstruck as the rest of them.

"Who's Douglas Kinnaird?" Molly placed her fingers on her temples. "I've heard that name before."

"He was the mayor here until he died two years ago. Heart attack." Hamish had wandered downstairs. He grabbed the letter before anyone could stop him. "Now then, what's this all about?"

4

Molly expected Hamish to explode into a Gaelic tirade that would make his earlier rants seem bland as porridge.

Instead, he said, "Could be some silly prank. Still, given the break-in, I'm thinking you should call the police."

Molly and her partners groaned. After mere days of ownership, they'd have to call the police *again?*

"Do you have any idea who would write something like this?" Carol asked.

Hamish shrugged. "None. But foolish folk abound, even in a town like Loch Mallaig."

"Maybe this has something to do with the burglary," Molly suggested.

"That's for the police to determine." He carefully placed the letter back in the cabinet. "I imagine they'll want to check it for fingerprints, so let's leave it until they come."

Hamish turned and looked pointedly at Molly.

She couldn't help fidgeting as though under the scrutiny of a stern schoolteacher—which technically she was. Then she realized that he expected her to place the call to the police. Hamish owned a cell phone but rarely carried it, so she pulled her own from her jeans pocket.

The receptionist who answered Molly's call about the suspicious letter peppered her with follow-up questions. "At the old Bailey Funeral Home? Goodness gracious, you just had a break-in, didn't you? Who was it from? What did the letter say?"

"Um . . ." The rapid-fire interrogation scattered Molly's thoughts, but she knew better than to blurt sensitive details to this person who appeared anything but closemouthed.

Molly caught sight of a small smirk on Hamish's face as he headed back to work. *He knew exactly who would answer my call.*

"You're all from out of town, aren't you?" the receptionist continued. "Going to start up the funeral parlor again? I'm not sure that's a good idea. After all, we still have Fitzgerald's, and people around here may not want to entrust their loved ones to outsiders."

Carol frowned questioningly at Molly, who shrugged and tapped her thumb and fingers together to indicate that the person on the other end of the line wouldn't stop talking. Carol shook her head and mouthed, "Ask for Gillespie."

It took several attempts, but Molly finally persuaded the woman to connect her with the deputy chief. His level voice calmed the tempest in Molly's stomach. After listening in blessed silence, Gillespie told her he couldn't come immediately, but would send Officer Anderson as soon as possible.

As Molly hung up, Carol put her hands on her hips. "I'll bet that was Wilma Guthrie, the police department's receptionist. When she called about the break-in, I practically had to bribe her to get through to Gillespie. Sorry I didn't warn you."

"No need to apologize," Molly said. "An officer will be here shortly."

Officer Greer Anderson, a thirtysomething, personable woman whose efficient air rivaled Gillespie's, arrived less than fifteen minutes later. After welcoming them to the community, she said, "I'm sorry you're having to deal with difficulties like this before you even open. We hope you'll stay."

"We intend to," Laura assured her.

Molly, who had feared Laura would revert to her former pessimism about the "creepy old house," liked the sound of that.

Officer Anderson questioned the three partners and Hamish in the kitchen after they showed her where the envelope had been discovered. She dusted the cabinet for fingerprints, requesting they refrain from further work on it until the results emerged, then put the letter in a plastic evidence bag.

As she watched the procedure with Laura and Carol, Molly asked, "Could you tell us a little about Douglas Kinnaird?"

A shade of reserve passed over Anderson's face. "He was our mayor for several terms until he passed away a couple of years ago. Heart attack."

Her cool demeanor didn't surprise Molly. As a town employee, the officer wouldn't discuss her former boss. Actually, Molly had hoped that Hamish, presented with an opportunity to flaunt his knowledge, would chime in with more information.

Instead, he grunted, "Are we done here? I have work to do outside before it snows again."

Officer Anderson nodded. "Sure. If we need to ask any of you more questions, we'll contact you."

While Hamish stomped out through the back door, Carol and Laura returned to the task of painting the cabinet interiors. Anderson, phone to ear, exited the kitchen and headed for the front door. Molly realized that she'd left her own phone in the main room, and as she went to retrieve it, she couldn't help but hear most of the officer's conversation echoing throughout the empty space.

"Hennie? Greer Anderson here."

How many Hennies lived in Loch Mallaig? Surely she was talking to Hennie Bailey.

"I'm at your old place. Yes, I know you already talked to Gillespie about the break-in, but the new owners have found a letter." After a pause while Hennie spoke, Anderson continued, "It raises some questions about a person in the past." Another pause. "I'd rather not say who. Do you remember receiving an envelope and stuffing it in a cabinet, maybe?" The officer held up the bagged letter and stared at it. "I was afraid you'd say that. We're hoping it's somebody who's been watching too many movies." Silence returned for a few seconds. "I know, the new owners really don't need this. Thanks anyway, Hennie. I appreciate your time."

As Anderson disconnected the call, she made eye contact with Molly, who grimaced sheepishly.

"Sorry, I was just getting my phone." Molly held up her own mobile phone. "I didn't mean to eavesdrop."

"It wasn't exactly a top secret call," Officer Anderson said with a warm smile. "We'll get back to you as soon as we know something." Her expression turned sympathetic. "Just keep on doing what you're doing. This time next year, you—and the rest of Loch Mallaig—will be glad you did."

"Thank you, Officer," Molly said as she went to the front door to see her out.

Molly watched Anderson walk toward her cruiser, then glanced around the front porch, expecting to spot Hamish working away in a far corner. She'd seen him there earlier, repairing gingerbread trimming.

But there was no sign of their cranky handyman, even as Molly peered through side windows to other areas of the porch.

Had Hamish disappeared?

Tiny fingers of fear slithered up her back.

Molly thumped her head. *For heaven's sake, why am I letting all this get to me?* The fast-moving Hamish had probably already moved on to another task. He'd gone out the back door, after all.

Keep on doing what you're doing. With Greer's words steadying her, Molly strode into the kitchen hallway to join her friends.

She nearly ran over Hamish, who didn't issue a torrent of reproach, not even a "Hen, watch where you're goin.'"

His usually animated face was frozen, a screwdriver clutched in his hand.

How long had he been standing there, silent as a stone? He might have heard Officer Anderson's conversation with Hennie, but she hadn't revealed anything he didn't already know.

Hamish said nothing now, only headed back to the front porch, his face like a statue's.

It wasn't like the volatile handyman to suddenly be stoic.

Molly scolded her unruly imagination again, but she couldn't help but wonder—did Hamish know more about this letter than he was saying?

Laura's moving day offered Molly and her partners a break from complications at the bakehouse. It also guaranteed a few more creaks in their already aching backs. Someday, Molly promised herself, the heaviest thing they'd be lifting would be boxes of cream puffs.

Laura had leased a picturesque stone cottage from a retired tax attorney named Alastair Thomson and his wife, Jane. They had helped her line up a small rental truck at an excellent price and even offered the services of their own big pickup to haul Laura's belongings from the storage unit she'd rented while the cottage was being vacated by the previous tenant.

The Thomsons were clearly generous, helpful folks—but perhaps a little too helpful? As Molly, Carol, and Harvey watched Laura and her landlords open the storage unit, Molly worried that, before day's end, they would be taking the septuagenarian couple to the emergency room.

When Fergus joined them, she whispered, "Do you think we should suggest the Thomsons drive ahead to the cottage?"

"Sounds like a good idea to me," Carol murmured, apparently sharing the same concern.

Fergus chuckled. "If you're afraid they'll hurt something, don't give it a second thought. Alastair's a first-class caber tosser."

Molly frowned. "A what?"

"A log thrower. And a good one at that." Fergus grinned. "He's beaten me out of first place a couple of times during the Scottish Games Festival."

Perhaps Laura's modest piles of boxes wouldn't present a problem for Alastair after all. Molly watched Fergus's eyes widen, though, when Hamish and Joyce drove up in their green 1955 Studebaker Speedster.

"Are they planning to help today?" Fergus asked under his breath.

"Laura accepted all the help she was offered." Carol cocked her head. "Is something wrong?"

Instead of answering, Fergus hurried to the storage unit. He said something to Jane, then slapped Alastair on the back, talking and laughing a little too loudly.

Petite Jane, nearly swallowed by her furry parka, skittered over the snow like a squirrel. She hugged Joyce and blurted, "How wonderful to see you. We haven't talked in ages."

Though seemingly not as delighted, Joyce nevertheless returned the hug and greeting, keeping a glowering Hamish behind her.

Was this a new complication? Molly closed her eyes for a two-second prayer. *Heaven help us.* Opening her eyes, she wondered if she really wanted to know what this peculiar behavior was all about. Still, when Carol gestured toward the tense little group, Molly followed her and Harvey, mentally scrolling for topics that might make for light, easy conversation.

Hopefully, no one would mention the break-in or letter.

Of course, Jane did.

"It was so sweet of everyone to come and help these poor girls—what with dangerous criminals smashing their windows and leaving letters written in blood lying around." Jane wrinkled her elfish face. "Disgraceful, that's what it is."

Molly stifled a groan. Obviously, several versions of the bakehouse events were circulating in Loch Mallaig. At least Jane didn't appear to know the letter involved the late mayor—yet.

While Molly and Carol did their best to direct the chitchat back to comments on good moving weather and hopes for an early spring, Joyce slipped her arm through her husband's and gently tugged him toward the storage unit. Hamish followed, reluctance in every line of his body.

Jane, chattering away, didn't appear to notice. Molly divided her attention between the conversation and Hamish, whose glare was fixed on the storage unit.

As the Bruces approached, Alastair turned from Fergus and crossed his arms, eyes glinting like blue ice as he focused on Hamish. "Well now, you're free on this fine day? I would think you'd be out watching the birds around the lake."

Hamish bristled. "Been watching them all winter, the ones that stay. Hoping to see lots more this *spring.*"

Birds? Spring? Why should those subjects ignite the older men's tempers? Molly cast a confused glance at Fergus, who appeared tense but trying to hide it.

"I can't wait until spring either." A small, wicked grin crossed Alastair's face. "The Piping Yoopers are ready to make music too, louder and stronger than ever before."

Hamish's face reddened.

Before Molly could begin to make sense of this bizarre exchange, Joyce announced, "We are here to help, not talk." She steered her husband into the storage unit, where an oblivious Laura was gleefully organizing which furniture and boxes would go first.

Although Molly wondered fleetingly if Laura should simply hire movers who didn't hold mysterious grudges against each other, she joined everyone else in the task at hand. As they worked, tensions seemed to relax, and they quickly loaded the trucks, then unloaded at the cottage without serious damage to furnishings or egos.

Molly marveled at Jane's and Joyce's vitality. Having coped with the Upper Peninsula's harsh weather and often limited resources as they'd raised their families, nothing seemed to slow them.

"These UP women are something else," Molly whispered as she and Carol unpacked dishes in the cottage kitchen. "Maybe by the time we're their age, we'll be that tough."

On the other hand, Molly hoped she wouldn't adopt the small-town pastime of gossip that grew weird rumors like mold on bread. Joyce seemed to have escaped the scourge. While they worked, she updated them on current happenings around town, yet avoided dishing up dirt. Jane, however, threw in a few juicy bits of conjecture about fellow Loch Mallaig citizens—especially those in town government—that Molly decided to forget.

When Jane began talking about the village's late mayor, though, Molly listened intently.

"Douglas Kinnaird was the most wonderful mayor," Jane gushed. "Not surprising since he was descended from the town's founders, after all. He could tell a story that would make you laugh until it hurt. Why, he took tea almost every afternoon at Neeps and Tatties just so we could share our thoughts. Mayor Doug really cared. We'll never have another one like him again. Never."

"He certainly sounds like a man of the people," Carol said.

"Oh yes. Even when he threw parties on his boat, he didn't just invite the higher-ups, you know. He made sure no one was left out." Jane offered a beatific smile. "And he often visited town organizations, like the senior club, after-school groups, even preschools. Those little darlings simply loved him. My granddaughter used to cry when he had to leave."

"He sounds like a busy man," Molly said as she unwrapped Laura's coffee maker. "Did he have a family?"

Jane nodded. "A lovely family. His wife, Fiona, and one son, Charlie. A kinder husband and father you never saw."

"He was one of the most likable people you'd ever meet," Joyce agreed, "but Tavish Calhoun is also an excellent mayor. I'm thankful he was willing to step in as interim after Mayor Kinnaird passed away. It wasn't surprising that he won the election."

"But Tavish was a dentist." Jane winced, as if feeling his probe. "You have to make an appointment to see him. He never takes tea at Neeps and Tatties the way Mayor Doug did." She pursed her lips. "My grandchildren don't even know his name."

"I'm sure every mayor has their own way of governing," Carol said diplomatically.

"Mayor Doug worked hard to attract new businesses to Loch Mallaig, but Tavish scares them away." Jane's green eyes glinted behind her glasses. "I heard he told a major chain store that we didn't want them to come here. And they decided to build their new store elsewhere."

"Now, now, lass, you know that's just a rumor." Alastair, who had entered unnoticed, plopped two more boxes on the kitchen counter. "And don't you think there are enough rumors flying around town without adding to them?"

"We'll see if it's just a rumor," Jane snapped. Nevertheless, her husband's soothing yet potent question seemed to still the wind in her sails, as she left local politics alone the rest of the day.

Despite occasional flares of tension between Hamish and Alastair, which Fergus reliably stepped in to quell, they accomplished far more than Molly had expected. As she helped haul in the last boxes, Molly took a moment to appreciate the historical stone cottage that had once been inhabited by crofters, or tenant farmers. Not far from Fergus's resort, the quaint lakeside dwelling had been built on the original Castleglen estate, though the parcel had been divided long ago. With a smile, Molly pictured Laura's antiques—cherished pieces inherited from her grandmother that had been lying in wait in her parents' basement for years—decorating the cottage, and she knew that it was the perfect home for her dear friend.

Finally, the senior helpers declared the end of their workday. Long after they left, Laura continued zipping around, unpacking this, arranging that, taking pictures of everything and commanding everyone to smile for selfies.

After the latest group photo, Harvey flopped onto a sofa. "Wake me up when you've decided whether the pink teapot looks better on the right or left side of the mantel."

Laura clasped her dusty hands, her expression apologetic. "Oh my, please feel free to go home. I couldn't sleep now if I wanted to, but you all must be exhausted."

Molly summoned the strength for a hug, then joined Carol, Harvey, and Fergus as they departed in the snowy twilight. The cottage's narrow driveway had barely accommodated the trucks, so they had all parked on the street. Though she was staying with the MacCallans, Molly had driven her own vehicle to help transport some of Laura's belongings.

As they walked, Molly glanced at Fergus. "Would you mind explaining about the birds and spring?"

He stared at her in confusion for a moment, then laughed heartily. "I suppose someone should. It all has to do with bagpipes."

"Bagpipes?" Molly echoed.

Fergus nodded. "Yeah, Hamish hates them."

"But Hamish claims he's descended from Robert the Bruce," Carol protested. "How can he hate bagpipes?"

"Well, maybe not so much bagpipes as the way they interfere with his birds," Fergus clarified.

"And how do they interfere?" Molly asked.

"Hamish is a fanatical bird-watcher. During the warm months, he goes for a walk every evening to study them." Fergus cocked his head. "Do you remember hearing bagpipes back during those summers you came to Loch Mallaig?"

Molly had forgotten, but at his words, memories flooded back of the skirling tones she'd considered such an integral part of the small town. They'd colored every sunset... *Oh.* "I take it the bagpipes bother the birds?"

"According to Hamish they do. And guess who plays those bagpipes every sunset in spring, summer, and fall?" Fergus's tone was even, but there was a twinkle in his eye.

"Alastair." Looking heavenward, Carol clucked her tongue.

Molly sighed. "And I suppose neither stubborn man wants to compromise a teensy-weensy bit?"

"Not even a microscopic bit." Fergus shook his head. "Not only that, but Alastair—the head of the bagpipe club, The Piping Yoopers—is planning several outdoor concerts this year. At sunset, of course."

They all chuckled, then wished each other good night and climbed into their respective cars. As she dropped into the driver's seat of her silver Honda Fit, Molly made a mental note to avoid bringing up anything regarding birds or bagpipes with Hamish in the future . . . although she fleetingly wondered if one needed any bagpiping experience to join The Piping Yoopers.

Clouds of snowflakes obscured her view through the windshield on the way back to Carol's, but not as much as whirling thoughts muddled her mind.

Don't you think there are enough rumors flying about town without adding to them? Alastair's no-nonsense voice reminded her.

Despite her weariness and echoes of Alastair's warning, Molly tried to make sense of the growing jumble of puzzle pieces she'd accumulated since arriving in Loch Mallaig. The two her brain seemed most fixated on were the death of former mayor Douglas Kinnaird and the political moves of his successor, Tavish Calhoun—did those pieces fit together?

5

Thanks to her mind's manic workings robbing her of sleep, Molly felt like a moving truck had run over her the next morning. If only someone would place her on a dolly and haul her to breakfast.

Not going to happen. Molly dragged herself from the warm quilts and trudged her way to Carol's cozy kitchen.

Her hostess appeared equally groggy. "Guess we're really missing Laura this morning. I could use some of her energy right now."

"But she's only a few miles away," Molly said, though the idea didn't bring much comfort. "It's not as if she's back in New York."

"I know." Carol sighed. "Still, it's been so much fun to be together again."

"We'll be together again soon—stripping that awful wallpaper from the upstairs kitchen." Could Molly face those cows this morning? She couldn't help but shudder.

Diplomatic Carol kept silent, but her face said it all.

Harvey, bundled against the cold morning, entered through the back door and slammed it shut. "You girls look like you're headed to a funeral."

"We are going to a funeral parlor." Carol reached for her old gray-and-white-striped cat, Pascal, as he approached his food dish, but the rarely seen feline ducked under her hand and went for his breakfast from a different angle.

Harvey placed a small basket on the counter. "I'm sore too, but a couple of fresh eggs apiece will perk us up." After hanging his coat on a hook, Harvey proceeded to fry the eggs he'd found in their new chicken coop, pairing them with spicy pork sausage patties that made Molly's mouth water.

"I know what else will make you feel better," Harvey said as Molly dropped English muffins into the toaster. "Angus."

Instead, her heart clenched and her eyes moistened. "Angus?" The logical part of Molly's brain knew it was silly to miss her Scottie so much when he was only forty miles away—but the rest of her longed to cuddle him tight. "The kennel told me he's just getting used to their routine. I'm not sure a visit's a good idea."

"Who said anything about a visit?" Carol's face had brightened. "We've decided you and Angus have been apart long enough. Bring him here. Today."

Molly stared. "But Pascal—"

Carol waved away her protests. "Pascal's an introvert. He spends ninety-five percent of his time under our bed anyway."

Harvey nodded. "Yep. If we close the door on him, he'll love it."

As if to confirm her words, the big tom padded down the hall and disappeared into the master bedroom.

Angus, on the other hand, nearly turned somersaults when the kennel assistant led him out to Molly in the waiting area. Barking his joy, he wiggled from nose to tail as she buried her face in his black fur, and his elation instantly rubbed off on her.

"You're coming to work with me, boy," Molly told him as she gathered up his leash. "I need your moral support to tackle that wallpaper."

Angus yipped approval, then followed her out to her car and snuggled as close to her as possible for the hour-long drive to Bread on Arrival. He sniffed merrily as she led him up the sidewalk and through the front door.

Hamish strode in from the back door and stopped dead in his tracks when he saw Molly wiping Angus's paws in the entry. The handyman's face darkened. *Oh no you don't.* A hot flush crept up Molly's face. *This is my business. My dog. If Angus wants to paint my apartment using his tail, that's our choice.*

Molly unclipped the dog's leash, summoned a smile, and stood. "Hi, Hamish. This is my dog, Angus. He'll stay upstairs with me."

Angus sat at Molly's feet and gazed up at her adoringly, wagging his tail and panting blithely with the knowledge that he was being discussed.

Hamish harrumphed. "If he gets underfoot or chews my brushes—"

"Then I'll reimburse you and have him stay at Carol's," Molly finished. "But Angus is more polite than many people. It takes a lot of effort to resist his charms." She whistled for the Scottie as she headed upstairs.

He bounded after her and received a royal welcome from Carol and Laura, who had already begun steaming and stripping away the bovine wallpaper.

"I'm loving that smile on your face," Carol said as she hugged Molly, and Laura followed suit.

"Angus is just what I needed." Molly fished a treat out of her bag and tossed it to him.

He caught it neatly and then pranced over to a spot near a window. He settled and crunched the biscuit while basking in fresh sunbeams that had broken through the clouds.

His presence in the outdated, messy apartment made Molly feel like it could truly become home.

"I wonder if the Baileys were gardeners," Carol said wistfully as she peered out the apartment's frosty windows a while later. "Hard to tell if there are any perennials buried under the snow."

"Perennials?" Laura raised a dubious eyebrow. "As in green plants?"

Molly grinned at Carol. "I know you're an optimist, but—"

"When it snows in April, you've got to focus on spring. I might call Hennie and ask about the yard's layout." Carol gave the other women a sideways look from under her long, black lashes. "I might also mention the letter."

Laura's smooth forehead wrinkled. "Hennie already told Officer Anderson she didn't know anything about it."

"But Hennie's had time to think about it," Carol said. "Maybe she remembers details she didn't recall the other day, details she still thinks unimportant."

"You're right, of course." For a moment, Molly forgot about wallpaper. "Casually mentioning it during a chat about tulip beds might accomplish more than a police interview."

"I'm glad you've got a green thumb." Laura gave Carol's arm a gentle poke. "If I tried that approach, Hennie would sniff out in a second that I don't know a daffodil from a dandelion."

Carol went downstairs to retrieve Hennie's phone number. When she returned, she'd already placed the call and been invited over to get the flower bed map Hennie had meant to give the trio at the closing.

Having worked nonstop all day, Molly and Laura decided to knock off a little early too.

"I could always use an extra hour to lavish on my new home," Laura said.

"Your energy knows no bounds," Molly said as she scrubbed paint from her hands. "I think I'll head to the library. I've been wanting to visit."

Laura gave her a knowing look. "Going to check out the mayors?"

Molly nodded. "What percentage of Jane Thomson's version of their rivalry is purely Jane's version? I'd like to know."

"Good," Carol affirmed. "We need to know the facts if we're going to make headway on that letter."

As they donned coats to leave, Angus danced around their ankles. *Angus.* Molly couldn't leave him in the car while she did research. "Carol, would Harvey mind if I dropped Angus by? He won't be a bother. After all the excitement today, he'll likely curl up and sleep."

"Harvey would probably welcome the distraction," Carol said. "He's working on a story that's giving him fits." As a retired journalist, Harvey wrote occasional articles for online news outlets and also did freelance work for outdoor magazines.

"What's it about?" Laura asked as she buttoned her coat.

"Canadian hunters who come to the States to avoid their country's gun restrictions." Carol sighed. "I understand why none of them want to talk to Harvey. But it does make this particular job difficult."

Molly reconsidered. "Are you sure leaving Angus with him won't be a bother?"

"He'll probably keep Angus awake just so he can leave his laptop."

True to Carol's promise, Harvey welcomed the Scottie with open arms. After warmly greeting Harvey, however, Angus opted to stay close to his owner when Molly decided to do a quick Internet search on her own computer before going to the library. The Scottie followed at her heels to the guest room and lay on her feet as she typed—not a bad thing, as his furry presence warmed her toes.

Opening her laptop, she checked her e-mail. A good friend from

Chicago had sent her a message with the subject line *Bet you'll be doing this soon* that contained a link to a Scottish dance video. She watched the video, then clicked a few more links suggested by the browser.

For the life of her, Molly couldn't figure out the difference between a fling and a jig. Though she jogged at least twice a week and considered herself in decent shape, the dancers' coordination and stamina made Molly feel ancient.

Dallis Witherspoon might focus his charming smile on me for a decade, but no way will I try that in public.

After sending a jovial response to her friend, Molly turned her attention to finding information on Loch Mallaig's recent mayors. Sure enough, even the newspaper in nearby Marquette had noted Mayor Kinnaird's death from a heart attack after a town council meeting, as Officer Anderson had told them. The paper even posted an extensive obituary that listed his accomplishments. However, Loch Mallaig's local paper, the *Crown Press News,* and those of surrounding small towns didn't publish their older articles online, so she learned no other details.

Knowing she'd probably find far more at the library, she donned her parka again, steeling herself for a difficult departure.

Sure enough, Angus fixed pathetic eyes on her as she grabbed her purse but not his leash. Molly was just debating whether to stay when Harvey offered Angus a taste of leftover bacon from the fridge.

The Scottie barely glanced at Molly when she left.

So much for his pining away. Molly grinned as she headed for the old brick building downtown.

The Loch Mallaig Library's elegant but musty interior reflected the cornerstone's inscription that it had been built in 1901. The first thing she saw when she entered through the heavy, brass-knobbed inner doors was a large card catalog, making her wonder if the library even owned a computer.

Beyond the card catalog, a stout, gray-haired woman stood behind an old-fashioned wooden counter, which featured a large sign demanding cell phones be silenced. The lady's shrewd green eyes attached to Molly the minute she walked in. "Welcome. I'm Grizela Duff, the head librarian here. You are one of the new bakers in town."

It was a statement, not a question, and it was delivered in an authentic Scottish accent, thicker than the faint burr many residents spoke with.

"We're always glad to see new readers," Grizela continued, extending her hand. "Can I help you find a good novel to enjoy by the fire?"

"I'd love that. And my name is Molly Ferris." Molly shook the librarian's strong hand. Did Grizela harbor strong opinions too? Given the century-old air of the place, Molly decided not to ask about computers. "First, could you show me your reference section? I'd like to read up a little on the town's history and look through newspapers from the past ten years or so."

"Oh?" Grizela's eyes glinted, and Molly felt as if the woman were x-raying her thoughts. "Follow me, please." She guided Molly to the opposite side of the large room and pointed to dustless shelves full of thick books. "The town history is preserved in those volumes. You'll find we keep accurate records—*Haud yer wheesht!*" she hissed suddenly.

A startled Molly didn't know Gaelic, and maybe the giggling teens in a corner didn't either, but they all understood the librarian's crystal clear meaning. The girls fell silent, dropped their smiles, and resumed studying.

Grizela gave a satisfied nod and patted one of the old olive-green file cabinets nearby. "Here is where we keep clippings from a decade past to the present. If you wish to examine older articles, they're on microfiche."

Molly had already spotted the outdated machine. "Thank you. I've used one before." *More than thirty years ago, back in high school.*

She waited for the librarian to return to her desk, but it appeared that Grizela was in no hurry to go. "I am also president of the Loch Mallaig Historical Society. I'd be glad to answer any questions about our town. Perhaps you could tell me the subject you're seeking information about?"

Molly didn't want to tip her hand, but rather than rouse suspicion, she said, "I'm interested in local government, especially elections."

"Ah, you are in luck. You will find whatever you need in this drawer." Grizela's Scottish accent deepened, it seemed, with her interest. Within seconds, she'd retrieved a stack of manila folders that would keep Molly busy for a week straight.

Providing the wealth of information seemed to satisfy the librarian, and she departed to find Molly a good novel to read.

Probably enough novels to last through summer.

Molly hurriedly flipped through the files, which contained minutes from town council meetings and detailed accounts of local elections—all of it so carefully arranged that Molly hesitated to disturb them.

Grizela's organization, however, made the next hour far more productive than Molly had anticipated. First, Jane's assessment of Mayor Douglas Kinnaird—at least, as far as popularity went—seemed fairly accurate. The newspaper rarely printed more than two consecutive editions without including a major article touting Kinnaird's latest meeting or event. Photos of the ruggedly handsome, often kilted mayor abounded: large pictures of him shaking hands with senior citizens, playing bagpipes at a town festival, holding an oversize check documenting his personal contribution to the town's food pantry. He'd even won a local bridie-eating contest, a competition in which stalwart locals consumed enormous numbers of Scottish meat-filled hand pies.

As Officer Anderson had indicated, Kinnaird had suffered a fatal heart attack after a town council meeting. The coverage of his obituary and funeral had continued for days.

They all but added a halo to his picture, Molly thought as she skimmed the fifth article in as many days regarding the mayor. Kinnaird had been elected to several terms as mayor. Tavish Calhoun had served as council president for a number of years. As long as the meetings involved no major changes in the town's government or business life, discussions and votes appeared fairly harmonious. Skimming page after page of dry summaries, Molly nearly drifted off to sleep.

However, when a fast-food chain had wanted to open a restaurant in Loch Mallaig five years earlier, a number of townspeople attended meetings, both supporting and opposing the change. Molly frowned over the list of names of those who'd spoken up, some of which sounded familiar. During subsequent meetings, Kinnaird had implied that Calhoun had delayed the chain's presentation, then council votes on the issue until the company finally canceled its plans.

Hadn't Jane mentioned a similar scenario with a department store chain? Molly dug in again, finding nothing during Kinnaird's term, but discovering that one indeed had approached the town council the previous November about building a new store in Loch Mallaig. She leafed through subsequent meetings again and again, but couldn't find a second mention of the project. Calhoun was mayor, but who was council president? Cameron MacPhee.

Oh yes, the Mac-something person who had stopped by Bread on Arrival to welcome Molly and her partners. Perhaps he agreed with Calhoun to keep chains out of Loch Mallaig, and therefore approved of a single-shop bakery moving in?

Her eye fell on an annual report that listed the mayor's pay—hardly enough to tempt Calhoun to murder Kinnaird for his position, especially as Calhoun had been a dentist with a comfortable income. Would he have killed Kinnaird to advance his anti-chain agenda? Or simply to gain power?

"My, but you're a dedicated one."

Molly jumped, almost colliding with Grizela's bent form above her. How long had the woman been reading over her shoulder?

Grizela stepped back. "I do hate to interrupt you, but we will close in five minutes."

"Oh my. I'm sorry. Goodness, the time has flown." Molly didn't usually babble, but Grizela made her feel like she'd been caught passing notes in grade school. Molly stood, sending several sheets flying.

Grizela caught them before they reached the floor. Her grip on the papers was gentle, but steel crept into her voice. "I do hope you found the information you were seeking."

"Most of it." Molly hadn't read the election accounts, but she knew she needed to gather her belongings and go before she committed any other unforgivable acts.

She couldn't hurry out the door, however, because Grizela loaded her up with a stack of novels. "I made you a temporary card," the mercurial librarian said, her tone now quite cheery. "And you'll be back within a week or so, won't you, dear? You can pick up the permanent one then."

Mumbling her thanks, Molly lugged the books toward the door, feeling the woman's gaze laser focused on her back. Did Grizela inspect every new citizen with such scrutiny?

Or only those interested in the machinations of Loch Mallaig's town government?

6

The next morning, as Molly and Carol prepared to swish the first paint onto her kitchenette's walls, they heard the unmistakable sound of whistling as footsteps ascended the stairs.

"Hamish?" Molly stared at her friend. Their handyman was not a morning person, and they normally didn't approach him until he'd finished every drop of the creamy tea in his thermos.

Hamish poked his head inside the door. "Och, it is a lovely day. The ducks know it too—a whole flock landed on the lake last night. A bonny sight."

So spring migration patterns improved his moods? He didn't even give Angus a skeptical glance as the dog nosed around the apartment. He merely continued whistling as he went to the storeroom to work.

Hamish had painted an entire wall when Laura arrived at the top of the stairs, a covered pan in her hands and a delicious cloud of fragrance surrounding her.

Molly sniffed. "Wow. You've already initiated the new oven?"

"You bet. What good is an oven if it just sits there, cold and empty?" Laura uncovered her dessert. "Ovens get depressed if they're not used."

Hamish, continuing in his buoyant mood, didn't gripe when they all stopped work to sample Laura's shortbread apple pie with its perfectly caramelized lattice top.

"When we finally finish your bakehouse, put me down for two of these," he told her.

More footsteps sounded on the stairs, then Fergus appeared, his gaze quickly landing on Laura's pie. "Tell me you can use some help this morning."

"Absolutely. First, fuel for the day." Laura handed him a plate bearing a generous portion.

They settled in the office, Fergus and Hamish on folding chairs and the three women lined up on a gently used sofa Joyce had donated. Molly wasn't sure they'd share another break like this together, so she launched into a report of her library findings.

The others nodded as they ate—except for Fergus, who seemed to forget all about the tantalizing pie in front of him.

A reminder dinged in Molly's mind. He hadn't been present when they found the letter. "Sorry, Fergus. I guess we haven't kept you in the loop."

"I heard rumors that you found everything from old love letters to a treasure map," he said. "But what is this about the mayors?"

Officer Anderson hadn't sworn them to secrecy, though confidentiality made sense. Molly tossed a questioning glance at the others, who nodded their consent for her to share, then explained the letter's contents.

When Molly finished, Fergus's eyes widened. "That's bizarre."

"We thought so too," Molly agreed. "We contacted the police, of course, but decided to do a little digging on our own as well."

Fergus shook his head. "You all believe Calhoun got rid of Kinnaird?"

"We don't suspect anyone yet," Carol said hastily. "This letter could be a farce. I spoke with Hennie Bailey yesterday, and she didn't have a clue who could have written it or why."

"We're just gathering information," Laura added. "Considering possibilities."

Fergus continued shaking his head. "I know they were opponents, but I can't believe anyone—let alone Tavish Calhoun—would get rid of Kinnaird. Have you found anything to substantiate that?"

"Not so far," Molly said. "I'd like to know a little more about the mayors. I'm overdue to have my teeth cleaned anyway, so I made an appointment with the younger Dr. Calhoun. His dad used to practice in that office, right?"

"Yes," Fergus said. "Some of Tavish's staff still works there."

"Maybe I'll see or hear something that will give us better insights into Mayor Calhoun. At least it's a beginning." Molly set her fork on her plate. "We need more details about Mayor Kinnaird's heart attack too. And about the special election."

Fergus shrugged. "There's nothing unusual about either, as far as I know. Most of the town knew Kinnaird had health problems, which he tended to downplay. His heart attack didn't surprise his doctor. As for Calhoun having a hand in his death? I have a hard time believing it."

"But is it possible that Douglas Kinnaird knew something damaging about Calhoun?" Molly pressed. "Something that might set him off?"

"Always possible, I suppose," Carol said, "though it doesn't seem likely in this case. When I asked Jenny about it, she said that she and Craig didn't necessarily agree with Kinnaird, but they liked and respected him. They feel the same way about Calhoun."

Molly grimaced. "The whole idea does seem like a long shot. But we have to consider every possibility, don't you think?"

Amid the others' nods, Fergus asked, "Any leads as to who wrote that letter?"

Carol edged forward on her cushion. "Maybe Harvey could do some digging. He misses the investigative style he used to do before he retired. Maybe he'll uncover something we can't."

"I sure hope so," Laura said as she stood and started gathering everyone's plates.

Molly's phone rang, and she stood to remove it from her pocket. It was a local number she didn't recognize. "Hello?"

"Mrs. Ferris, this is Chief Owen Thomson with the Loch Mallaig Police Department," said a deep voice. "I'm calling about the letter incident."

"Hello, Chief Thomson," Molly said, glancing at her friends. "Do you mind if I put this on speakerphone so my partners can join?"

"Certainly," he said, and Molly hit the speaker button just in time for his next sentence. "We didn't find any suspicious fingerprints on the cabinet. No fingerprints on your letter either, so I'm afraid that's a dead end. It appears to have been typed on an older computer, then printed, but that doesn't narrow things down much."

A wry chuckle went around the group.

"This could be a prank of some sort," the chief continued, "though I can't imagine why someone would try to upset Mayor Kinnaird's family with a trick like this."

"Especially two years later," Fergus put in.

"I'd still advise caution and discretion," Thomson said. "We want to avoid upsetting anyone if possible. Also, I'm not convinced that it was a coincidence you had a break-in right before you found the letter. Please keep your wits about you, and your eyes and ears open."

"That we will," Hamish said.

Molly had almost forgotten his presence—a first. Why was he so quiet?

Before this letter incident, Molly would have considered his silence golden. Now, however, his reticence might cover a multitude of clues as to what was really going on.

What would it take to unlock that stubborn Scot's thoughts?

Fergus's glance intersected hers, and he shook his head the slightest bit.

Molly understood his meaning. *Don't try to force things.* She answered with a miniscule shrug and nod. Hamish would open up when—and if—he chose.

As she helped Carol wash dinner dishes that evening, Molly was still pondering Hamish's odd, taciturn manner—and rejoicing that Harvey had agreed to delve into their mysteries. She was pulled out of her thoughts when the sound of Angus barking erupted from her phone. It was the custom tone Chloe had recorded and set to go off anytime she texted her mother.

"You're done drying plates." Carol snatched away her dish towel. "Go talk to your daughter."

Molly hurried into her bedroom and peered at the message. *Sorry I got upset, Mom.*

Dealing with a twentysomething was *so* much easier than with a teenager. Molly let her shoulders slump in relief that Chloe's icy reception to the news about Bread on Arrival was starting to thaw. She dashed off a reply. *I didn't mean to upset you. Just wanted to keep you in the loop.*

I know. I miss you.

Miss you too, honey. I love you.

Chloe replied with a single heart icon. That was all, but as Molly blew a silent kiss in the general direction of Milwaukee, warmth flooded her.

Warmth—and guilt.

Perhaps, her maddening conscience suggested, *you forgot to mention the break-in? And the letter?*

Surely that was way too complicated to share in a text.

If you truly want to keep Chloe in the loop, why don't you call her?

"Because she'd worry herself sick if I told her," Molly argued aloud. "That wouldn't do anyone any good, would it?"

Molly hurried back to the kitchen, but Carol had already finished the dishes. Wanting to work out some nervous energy, Molly snapped a leash onto a very excited Angus. She donned her parka and led him out of the house for a walk, knowing full well that she wouldn't be able to outpace the jumble of troubled thoughts clogging her brain.

Despite her one long-ago attempt at knitting resulting in a sweater fit for an alien, Molly somehow found herself attending a meeting of the Fair Knitting Ladies, Loch Mallaig's knitting group, a few days later. Laura and Carol had already joined, and they'd convinced Molly to come along to that evening's gathering in the interest of digging up more information about Mayor Kinnaird's death.

Owned by Aileen Morrison and situated right next door to Bread on Arrival, The Knit Hoose's cheerful walls lined with skeins of many-colored yarn lifted Molly's spirits. At the back of the large room, comfy chairs surrounded a fireplace glowing with a fragrant fire—a welcome sight for three women who had spent the day ripping out old carpet and hauling it to the curb.

"You came!" Beverly Scott flashed her face-wide smile as Molly hung her coat beside Laura's and Carol's.

"So glad you could join us," Jane Thomson chirped.

Molly's aching muscles loosened as she sat, warmed by the fire and agreeable chitchat. Jane, she found out, was Chief Thomson's mother.

Jane beamed. "He wanted to be a policeman in Loch Mallaig when he was a little boy, and now he is."

Everyone had just settled in with hot cider, yarn, and needles—Molly had decided to knit a very simple scarf—when the bell over the front door jingled. Aileen rose to answer it, and a moment later, a familiar voice filled the room. The receptionist at the police station? Molly craned her neck.

A woman with dramatically teased red hair followed Aileen to their circle. Phone clasped to her ear and red-lipsticked mouth in high gear, she wiggled a hello with her fingers as she continued to talk.

When the newcomer finally disconnected her call, Aileen grabbed the moment and addressed Molly, Carol, and Laura. "Have you ladies met Wilma Guthrie?"

"Just on the phone," Molly said, then stood up with Carol and Laura to greet her.

"Oh my goodness, I've been wanting to meet you," Wilma said. "I think it's just terrible that someone would break into your business even before you open."

Molly grimaced at the mention of the break-in, but fortunately the loquacious Wilma and Jane promptly moved on to other topics. It became clear from the two women's nonstop chatting that both obviously cared deeply about their families and their town. The pleasant background hum might have made Molly drowsy, except that when it came to marrying-and-burying news, each tried to outdo the other.

Finally, Aileen shook her half-finished argyle sock at Wilma and Jane. "Stop it, you two. These girls don't have to hear the dating history of the whole town in one evening."

"Tell everyone about your bakehouse plans," Beverly urged. "My neighbor's daughter is getting married next Christmas. You're going to make wedding cakes, aren't you?"

Wilma's contributions to the conversation dropped off after that, especially since every few minutes, her phone squawked with an incoming call. Wilma spent so much time gabbing that when the group broke for coffee and strawberry meringues, Molly wondered why she'd come. Had she knitted even one row?

The receptionist didn't apologize in the least, casually mentioning, "I'm related to Alexander Graham Bell—my maiden name was Bell—so what would you expect? It's in my DNA." Wilma texted with one hand while nibbling a meringue held in the other.

One reason for her presence soon became evident as they resumed their knitting. When she wasn't chattering on the phone, Wilma attempted not so subtly to probe Molly and her partners for information about the letter.

Information that no doubt would be broadcast throughout the entire Upper Peninsula, should they be so unwise as to share it.

Instead, Molly steered Wilma back to her job. "Fielding calls for the police department is one important job."

"Yes, I like working in the town hall. Never boring. You meet all kinds there, from prisoners to the high-and-mighties." Wilma pulled a compact from her bag and re-fluffed her already sky-high bangs. "One time, I got my picture taken with a senator."

"I'll bet you know more about the town's everyday workings than anyone," Laura said.

"You've got that right." Wilma reapplied her vivid lipstick.

"I'll have you know that I know the police chief better than you," Jane joked.

Wilma laughed. "I'll grant you that. But every day, I rub shoulders with the mayor and town council. I get to know their spouses and watch their children grow up. It's fun when they come to visit—though Mayor Calhoun never lets me give his grandkids candy, just like their dad. Dentists, right?" She clucked her tongue and shook her head while the others laughed.

"Did Mayor Kinnaird's family come by too?" Molly ventured.

"Not that often." Wilma's smile faded. "He served as mayor longer than anybody else, but I didn't get to know Fiona very well. And their boy, Charlie—well, he just never said much. Never smiled much either, even when he was a toddler."

Jane's eyes flashed. "He's just the quiet type."

Rats. Molly realized she'd skipped a stitch. And just when Wilma was starting to leak interesting information, she'd ruffled Jane's feathers.

Aileen hastened to soothe Mayor Kinnaird's ardent supporter. "Charlie's always been very bright, though a bit solitary. He just happens to take after Fiona, not Douglas."

"Charlie's had a very difficult time, these past two years." Jane's glare hadn't diminished. "Does everyone expect a young man to get over the death of a father—such a dear father—overnight?"

Everyone agreed that wasn't to be expected, then Aileen changed the subject to everyone's plans for Easter.

When Jane had to leave early, Molly dared broach the subject of the Kinnaird family with Wilma again. "I wish I could have met him. From all I've heard, everyone in Loch Mallaig adored him."

"They did." Wilma leaned forward, lowering her voice. "Everyone but Charlie."

"Did they ever argue?"

"Not at the town hall. Not out loud, anyway—except one time, not long before the mayor's death." Wilma's eyes gleamed as she whispered, "I thought Douglas was about to raise a hand against the boy."

"How awful." Molly didn't have to fake her distress. "I hope that wasn't the last time Charlie saw his dad before he died."

Wilma brushed away the possibility with a red-nailed hand. "I'm sure it wasn't. The mayor didn't have his heart attack until a month later. But it was the last time Charlie showed up at town hall."

Wilma's ringtone broke into the conversation again, but this time, the sound had competition. A skirl of bagpipes pierced the shop walls. Wilma fled to the back hallway to hear her call.

Aileen set down her knitting needles and stood quickly. "The first sunset concert of the year. Jane said Alastair's been waiting forever for this day." She motioned to the others to follow her to the front of the shop, then opened the door.

Molly loved bagpipes, but the music had risen to almost deafening levels.

Their tartans brilliant against the dingy snow, at least a dozen members of The Piping Yoopers—Molly recognized Officer Anderson among them—stood at attention with the sun's golden beams as a backdrop. Townspeople left warm houses and businesses to watch and listen as The Yoopers, accompanied by two enthusiastic drummers, played the wild, joyous strains of *Scotland the Brave*. Several rosy-cheeked children, though bundled against the cold, danced like spring lambs on the sidewalk.

Dallis Witherspoon, clad in his typical exercise clothes, joined the youngsters. Muscular arms raised high, he jumped and spun as his feet moved in a blur. Molly watched in awe, as the man's vertical leap rivaled that of a basketball star. Despite lack of kilt or tartan, auburn-haired Dallis personified all the powerful grace of a Scottish warrior.

Molly marveled as several other townsfolk, including one energetic old lady, joined in the Scottish flash mob. "Can you believe Dallis actually thinks we'll join his dance group?" she asked Laura, who stood beside her. "I could never, ever learn that."

Laura shook her head. "Me neither."

"Please don't worry your heads about that." Aileen hastened to reassure them. "Just enjoy. It's the first frolic of spring—one to simply warm the heart."

And warm hearts it did. Clapping along with the others, Molly let the music and dancing swirl through her in a joyous flood.

Two faces, however, did not reflect the evening's celebration.

Hamish, hunched as if against a tempest, stood at the edge of Dumfries Park. Molly could see his scowl from a block away.

Another face, a young man's, stood out from the crowd across the street as Alastair played a final solo, *Amazing Grace*. The youth's haunted, dark eyes held Molly's for a moment, then wrenched away.

"Does that young man in the peacoat live here?" Molly asked Aileen.

The shop owner nodded. "Oh yes. He was in college, but he's been home a while. That's Charlie Kinnaird."

7

The Bakehouse Three, as Fergus had tagged Carol, Laura, and Molly, reveled in the April thaw as they walked along the rocky shores of Loch Mallaig, the lake that shared the town's name. A breeze blew off the water, but it wasn't the same chilly wind they'd endured for the last few weeks. Instead, the air held a hint of warmth. Laura had proposed the outing to fill a gap of time between finishing work at the bakehouse and dinner with Hamish and Joyce at their home along with the couple's son, Logan, his wife, Tanya, and their four daughters.

Before they knew it, they'd walked farther from the Dumfries Park shoreline than they'd ever gone. Close up, the houses lining the lakeside path appeared even more luxurious than Molly had imagined.

She gestured at one that had been of modest size but now had the lumber framing of a sizeable addition on it. "Wow, someone's doing a major remodeling job. When they're done, that house will be bigger than all the others."

"It already looks like a castle," Carol agreed. "Boy, I'd hate to paint all the rooms in that house."

"Bite your tongue," Laura scolded. "We wanted to forget about work, remember?"

And for the most part, they did, simply enjoying each other's company for a blissfully relaxing hour before they arrived at the Bruces' door, which was answered by a surprisingly genial Hamish. Had small but mighty Joyce made him promise to be on his best behavior? As he welcomed them and gave them a tour, he certainly seemed more inclined to smile. And Molly was pleased to note that despite his still somewhat gruff exterior, the glances Hamish sent his wife's way betrayed that he remained smitten.

The Bruces' gracious, Classical Revival-style home, with everything in its place, presented a pleasant contrast to the still-chaotic bakehouse. Molly's jaw dropped at the sight of Joyce's music room, with its rich, patterned carpet and shining grand piano. "Anybody who touches an instrument in this room couldn't help but play beautiful music," she said in awe.

"Some of my students play wonderfully. The ones who practice." Joyce half-grinned, half-grimaced. "Others? Well, they haven't been inspired yet."

"You teach piano?"

"And violin." Joyce's brown eyes sparkled. "Maybe we can talk our granddaughters into playing something for us tonight."

"Aye, they've inherited Joyce's talents." Hamish's voice contained more than a hint of pride.

When the four girls, all with varied shades of red hair, and their parents arrived, the children took turns wrapping their grandfather around their little fingers.

Janine, the curly-haired, chubby two-year-old, could do no wrong in his eyes. Despite Joyce's announcement that dinner would soon be served, Hamish slipped Janine a wrapped taffy from his pocket. When the other three clamored for their share, he readily complied.

"I love you, *Seanair*," said Leah, the artful five-year-old.

With difficulty, Molly and the others smothered laughter as their grumpy handyman melted into a puddle.

Tanya, the girls' mother, allowed their doting grandfather a little leeway, but she and Logan insisted on good manners as everyone consumed Joyce's delicious trout amandine dinner.

Afterward, the two older girls, Courtney, aged ten, and Alannah, seven, played a charming piano-violin duet featuring variations on *Twinkle, Twinkle, Little Star.* A short while later, Logan and Tanya bundled up all four girls and carted them home to bed since it was a school night.

Despite Hamish's love affair with his grandchildren, he dropped into an armchair like a sack of stones. Joyce fortified him with a cup of extra-strong tea, apparently a post-grandchild tradition. Harvey, who had joined in romping with the girls, gratefully welcomed one as well.

During the conversation over decaf coffee and tea, Laura brought up their walk and the mansions they'd seen along the lake.

"Someone's doing major renovations on one of the smaller homes." Carol described it. "I'm surprised they attempted it this early in the spring."

"Oh, that's Mayor Doug's place," Joyce said, then wilted slightly. "Or rather Fiona's. When she came home from Europe last November—she'd traveled since his death—she couldn't wait to get started on the house."

An extended trip to Europe? An extravagant remodeling project? Grief took all forms—which Molly well knew as a widow herself—but she couldn't help wondering about this widow's spend-the-insurance-money response to her husband's death. Did it come closer to a celebration than mourning?

Judging from her partners' glances, they wondered the same thing.

To Joyce, however, Fiona's reaction made perfect sense. "For years, she'd poured her life into managing Doug's health—not easy, as he certainly wasn't any help. I'm glad Fiona got away for a while and then decided to come back home. Now she can make a fresh start."

As she drove everyone home, Molly voiced her questions about the Kinnairds. "I'm not sure what to believe. Jane thinks they were the perfect family. Wilma implied they weren't."

"Wilma impresses me as being a little extreme," Carol said.

"You think?" Laura sniffed. "She gets my vote for gossip queen."

"Joyce confirmed that Fiona had devoted her life to taking care of Kinnaird," Molly pointed out, "and Joyce seems to be the type who knows what she's talking about."

Carol shrugged. "I suppose having access to his medications makes Fiona a prime suspect."

"Charlie probably had access too," Molly said, "at least when he was home from college. I'll have to check whether that timing lines up with his dad's death." Recalling the boy's desolate eyes, Molly's stomach clenched. "I hope Wilma was exaggerating their quarrel."

After a brief stop at Laura's cottage to drop her off, Molly drove the MacCallans to their log home. Once inside, Harvey opened his laptop and delved into Charlie's public record. He found one arrest for vandalism at Halloween when Charlie was a teenager and another more recent arrest for trespassing, but that was all. An arrest record was an arrest record, but these sounded like minor infractions.

"I can check with a detective friend of mine in Traverse City tomorrow," Harvey said. "He has access to resources I don't. Still, I'll be surprised if anything turns up. This kid looks relatively clean."

Guilt nibbled at Molly's conscience. Maybe she was suspecting a young man whose mourning for his dead father had deteriorated into despair.

Or perhaps she and her partners were vilifying a widow who was trying to get her life back together.

Tomorrow, before her dentist appointment, she'd call Chief Thomson and ask him if she could drop by. Amid his updating her on their break-in and the letter, maybe she could feel him out about the coroner's report on Mayor Kinnaird's death.

"I was hoping to run into you again, Molly."

Ordinarily Molly wouldn't mind encountering a friendly young man like Dallis Witherspoon. Certainly, she welcomed a delay that would keep her out of the dentist's chair for a few more minutes. But as an event planner, Molly had done extensive PR work. She recognized a salesman's smile when she saw one.

"I've heard your bakehouse is really shaping up." Dallis fell into step beside her on the slushy sidewalk. "Even when I first dropped by, you'd made a huge difference in that old place."

"Thanks. It probably looks better than I think it does. Because I'm there all the time, all I see is the mess."

They chatted for a few minutes, then came Dallis's inevitable invitation to join The Leaping Lowlanders.

Molly nearly laughed out loud. After seeing that dance performance at the park, no way would she show this guy her non-moves. Still, she listened politely as Dallis made his pitch.

"We're starting practices for summer events. Most of the dances include beginners doing easy jig steps in the background while more advanced dancers do their thing out front. I'm sure you and your friends could master those background moves. Besides," Dallis added, flashing his winning grin, "a new business needs visibility. Our summer performances attract crowds of tourists. I'd be glad to publicize your new bakehouse from time to time."

This guy is too good. "You've got a point," Molly admitted, "but after you see my three left feet in action, you may not want to put me on a stage."

Dallis laughed. "I've heard that before. I've changed several nondancers' minds. Just think about it," he urged, then waved goodbye as Molly headed toward Dr. Patrick Calhoun's office.

Molly did think about it—for ten seconds. Unfortunately, her uncoordinated parents didn't dance and had never encouraged her to learn. She'd faked her way through a few high school formals, with sad results.

Pushing away the unpleasant memories, Molly entered the dental office and checked in at the front desk. She was soon called back to the hygienist's chair.

"I'm so glad you and the other bakers bought Bailey's." Betty Anderson, Dr. Calhoun's sixtyish hygienist, chattered cheerily as she took x-rays of Molly's mouth. "How's the remodeling going? Think you'll open soon?"

Mouth stuffed with spacers, Molly could only nod.

"It's a beautiful old place, and I hated to see it get run-down." Betty expertly removed the spacers. "And Dr. Tavish—Mayor Calhoun, I mean—is always happy to see small businesses move into Loch Mallaig."

"Didn't he practice here before he became mayor?" Molly asked, even though she knew the answer.

"For more than thirty years." Betty sighed. "I know our town needs him as mayor, and Dr. Patrick is a wonderful dentist, but we really miss Dr. Tavish."

As she probed and scraped, Betty went on to extol her former boss's virtues. He'd given up so much to serve Loch Mallaig, to make sure it remained a beautiful small town. He cared about its finances. He cared about education. "Why, Dr. Tavish donates his whole mayor's salary to the schools so they can buy all those fancy computers."

If true, such generosity didn't necessarily prove his innocence, but it seemed to speak well of Calhoun's character.

Molly accepted the paper cup of water the hygienist handed her. "It sounds like Loch Mallaig has been blessed with several good mayors. Though the last one died in office, didn't he?"

Betty's smile drooped. "Yes, Mayor Kinnaird died of a heart attack. They found him in a back hallway after a town council meeting."

"Did he focus on education too?"

Betty's lively hazel eyes glanced left, then right. She lowered her voice. "I don't like to speak ill of the dead, but I think Mayor Kinnaird focused mostly on himself." She sighed. "Fiona would have done so much better if she'd married Cameron."

"Cameron MacPhee, the council president?" Molly ventured.

"Yes, such a nice man." Betty brought up Molly's x-rays on a computer monitor. "The MacPhees and Fiona's family were neighbors for years, and very close. Cameron never married. Maybe he liked Fiona more than he let on. But she was stuck on Doug all through high school."

Dr. Patrick, the mayor's son, appeared at that moment to probe and scrape a little more, so Molly figured she'd extracted all the information she would this morning.

Though she hadn't exactly had to pull it out of Betty, Jane, or Wilma. Isolated in this Upper Peninsula town, some inhabitants seemed to have turned gossip into an art form. Certainly a major source of entertainment, if not always rooted in truth. But, then, what *was* the truth?

8

"What can I do for you, Mrs. Ferris?" Chief Thomson asked, appearing relaxed as he leaned back in his desk chair.

"Please, call me Molly," she said. "And I was just wondering if you had any update on that letter we found."

"We haven't gotten far, I'm afraid," he replied. "We asked Mrs. Bailey for a list of people to whom she'd given access to the funeral home after Jim died—as far as she could remember, of course. After all, she closed it well over a year ago. Besides, Hennie admitted they never locked the place if they went for coffee across the street or ran out for bread." He shook his head. "During their years in business, the Baileys let families come and go all the time. Finding out who left the letter could prove impossible."

"If Mayor Kinnaird's death was suspicious, do you have any suspects?" Molly knew she was treading on thin ice with her questions, but she pushed forward anyway.

"Well," Thomson said carefully, "in any case of potential foul play, family members would be among the first suspects to investigate. However, I called the coroner and checked his report again, but there's nothing there to suggest anything other than a bona fide heart attack. Everybody knew Doug had diabetes and heart disease. And he didn't take care of himself."

"But he still had enemies, didn't he?" Molly probed. "Even though he was popular?"

Chief Thomson stiffened slightly, and his expression blanked.

Of course. Molly chastised herself for not remaining cognizant of the fact that the chief now worked under Calhoun. Though she guessed Thomson had at least considered the Kinnaird-Calhoun political feud as suspect, any obvious focus on it might not be received well by the chief's current boss.

Knowing she'd better leave before she lost Chief Thomson's goodwill, Molly stood. "Carol, Laura, and I so appreciate your help. We're grateful Loch Mallaig has such a concerned police force."

"We're glad to help any way we can. Hopefully, we'll find some actual evidence soon that will steer us in the right direction."

Could total amateurs like her and her partners assist a professional in solving this odd impasse? Hastily leaving the town hall, Molly doubted it. But that didn't keep her from deciding to stop at the library before returning to Bread on Arrival.

As she approached the venerable building, though, her phone rang. Molly tensed. Chloe?

No. Molly's mother.

"Well, how are things up there in the wilds?" Unlike Chloe, Janet Kirkpatrick sounded cheery. "Snow still on the ground?"

"Some." Molly matched her tone as she ducked into the library's small entry. "Your daffodils are already blooming in Iowa, aren't they?"

"Earlier than we ever saw them when we were raising you in Ann Arbor, that's for sure," Janet chirped.

"We aren't too far behind," Molly said. "The other day, I saw the teeniest, tiniest crocus peek out of the ground by the porch steps."

"Are you sure it wasn't a snow mirage?" her dad teased, coming on the line. "I've heard Yoopers get a little peculiar by April."

As they talked, Molly couldn't help comparing this easygoing, speakerphone conversation with her parents to recent ones with Chloe. Janet and Daniel Kirkpatrick, who also cherished fond memories of their summers in Loch Mallaig, understood why Molly had moved there—granted, they wouldn't have minded if she'd chosen somewhere closer to Davenport, Iowa.

After a few minutes of banter, though, her mom abruptly asked, "Honey, have you been working too hard? You sound tired."

Molly cringed. "You sound tired" inevitably led to the "You're not telling me about something" discussion.

Something like a break-in? Molly's conscience yammered again. *And the letter?*

But why should she worry Chloe *or* her parents? "I'm fine, Mom. Yes, remodeling the bakehouse has proven to be a little more work than we expected, but it's already beautiful."

"Oh, send some pictures!" Janet exclaimed, her concerns about Molly's energy level evaporating.

"Of course, Mom."

Her dad cleared his throat. "Is the business side working out?"

"Actually, we're under budget," Molly told them proudly. "Carol keeps us in check. And Fergus helped us find an excellent handyman who's very reasonable."

"Fergus?" her mother lilted. "I always liked that boy."

Molly repressed a sigh, then told them about Hamish instead. She managed to finish the conversation without too many references to her old crush or accidentally revealing the odd troubles that had plagued her and her partners.

Molly finally disconnected the call and tossed the phone into her bag with a sigh. Playing the middle role, sandwiched between generations, was not for the faint of heart, especially when following a dream.

Right now, digging through stacks of boring papers and clippings sounded like a welcome reprieve. She pushed open the library's heavy door and saw Grizela at the front counter, inserting cards into recently checked-in books.

The librarian beamed. "I just knew we'd see you again soon, Molly. What can I do to help?"

Now familiar with the reference section, Molly wouldn't have minded digging on her own. However, when Grizela provided several folders of information that would save Molly hours of research, she welcomed them with open arms.

The town's statutes confirmed Calhoun's serving as interim mayor and his victory in the special election. In scrutinizing the election details, Molly found no hint of abnormality.

As she reviewed more pre-Calhoun town minutes, though, names Molly had passed over earlier began to stand out on the pages. Cameron MacPhee, whom her hygienist had touted as superior to Douglas Kinnaird, owned a drugstore. Even before serving on the council, he'd attended far more meetings than anyone else in Loch Mallaig, vehemently opposing Kinnaird's plans to recruit chain stores and restaurants. Tillie Campbell, Helga Hofmeister, Doreen Giobsan, and even Aileen Morrison had also attended to protest—not surprising, as their small shops could hardly compete with mega-retail prices and variety.

Could MacPhee or any of the others have had something to do with Kinnaird's death? Recalling Aileen's kind welcome as the head of the Fair Knitting Ladies, Molly would have been more inclined to vote her Ms. Congeniality. Still, when one's territory was threatened, sometimes primeval instincts took over even the gentlest of hearts.

Having decided she'd bounce a few ideas off her partners, Molly dug through newspaper accounts of Mayor Kinnaird's death—not only numerous writeups in the local *Crown Press News* and area weeklies, but also those in Houghton's *The Daily Mining Gazette* and Marquette's *The Mining Journal.* All appeared to have accepted the coroner's opinion without question.

Leafing through accounts written a few months later, Molly still found no trace of controversy about Kinnaird's death or confirmation of remaining hostilities. In fact, she saw one *Crown Press News* photo whose caption identified Fiona, the president of a gardening club, presenting a check for a park project to the new mayor, Tavish Calhoun, and Cameron MacPhee. Despite the fact that Fiona's husband had battled the two officials, the three appeared congenial. MacPhee, who towered over Fiona, even wore a big grin. Maybe he appreciated the publicity his drugstore was garnering?

Or was he still relieved that Kinnaird and his chain store dreams no longer threatened his business?

Slow down, Molly. She massaged her tightening temples. *You're reading entirely too much into every little thing.*

If only, as Chief Thomson had said, they could discover solid evidence. Evidence that would explain why someone would write that letter.

"Is there something else I can find for you?"

Grizela's voice, inches behind her head, startled Molly again. By now, she should have expected it.

Even as she flinched, she sensed the librarian stiffening. Had Grizela spotted something on the page before Molly? Something she shouldn't have seen?

When Molly turned to follow her helper's gaze, Grizela wasn't even looking Molly's way. Instead, she'd straightened. Her acidic gaze burned into a middle-aged, ponytailed man in a belted, knee-length coat made of tan leather who had just entered the library. Far from intimidated, the man smiled.

For a moment, Molly forgot about both mayors as Grizela swept toward the circulation desk. She stood in front of it, feet apart, as if ready to defend it with her life. "What do you want?"

The man's smirk widened. "Is that any way to greet a taxpayer who helps fund your job? Not very cordial of you."

Grizela sniffed. "If I thought you'd read one book in here, I might spare a hello. As it is, I won't waste one."

"My computer is down," he replied. "I wondered if I could use the library's computer for a few minutes."

The librarian crossed her arms. "I thought you once said it belonged in the Stone Age."

He shook his head, still smiling. "That was years ago. Surely you can forgive and forget after all this time?"

Grizela scowled, then turned her back to him and opened a door Molly hadn't noticed. It revealed what appeared to be her office, including a desk topped off with a large, outdated monitor that might have *preceded* the Stone Age.

"I'll need it in a few minutes," Grizela snapped, "so finish what you must and be gone." She busied herself with the stack of newly returned books on the counter.

Still wearing a grin, the man sauntered into the office as if he owned it.

As Molly neatly rearranged and stacked the materials she'd used, she heard an apparently ancient printer chug and clang. The man let loose a yell of frustration that sent Grizela storming into her office.

Even if Molly hadn't been near the completion of her research, she would have prepared to leave. How could anyone concentrate with the hot river of tension raging through the deceptively peaceful library? Molly returned her materials to the circulation desk and fled.

Note to self: never ask to use the computer. And never, ever cross Grizela Duff.

Not if you value your life.

9

"Thanks so much for your sermon, Reverend Findlay." Molly wasn't merely being polite as she shook hands with the fatherly, dark-haired pastor of St. Andrew's Church. She'd *needed* to hear God was with her. "It's been a challenging few weeks."

"I can imagine." Reverend Stuart Findlay shook his head. "If someone had burglarized the church during my first week—goodness, that's over twenty years ago—I might have backed out of the whole deal." His warm, dark eyes radiated sympathy. "We'll pray for better times ahead."

Better times will come. As Molly, Laura, and the MacCallans drank coffee and wandered the church's spacious foyer, Molly imagined her lovely, finished apartment and Bread on Arrival's grand opening, no shadows of burglary or mysterious letters darkening the picture.

It would happen. She knew it.

Beverly Scott and her husband, Ethan, chatted with them and introduced them to several friends. Molly feared she'd forget their names as quickly as she learned them, but she basked in their friendly welcome . . . until she sensed a different kind of gaze. Molly glanced over to see Cameron MacPhee in line to shake hands with the pastor a few feet away. But the unfriendly stare emanated from a petite, middle-aged brunette in front of him. Molly recognized the woman from her library research—it was Fiona Kinnaird.

The woman aimed a ladylike yet hostile glare at Molly. Or was Fiona staring at her partners? Molly couldn't quite tell.

Fiona's gaze cut away when Reverend Findlay turned his attention to her. "Good morning, Fiona. How's that remodeling project going?"

A smile brightened Fiona's sallow face. "Right on schedule. When it's finished, you and Bonnie must come for dinner and a tour."

"I'd love a tour. And I'm always up for dinner." The reverend grinned. "We're so glad you came back to Loch Mallaig."

As she listened to their conversation, Molly searched the crowd for Charlie, but there was no sign of him. She gulped half her coffee, as if that would help her make sense of everything. At this point, Molly and the others still considered the possibility of Mayor Kinnaird's murder theoretical. They'd agreed to keep suspects—including Fiona and Charlie—confidential. Yet Fiona had eyed them as if they were enemies.

Had she learned of their suspicions somehow? Or had Molly's imagination simply shifted into hyperdrive?

"What's with you?" Laura murmured. "You're awfully quiet all of a sudden."

Keeping her voice low to avoid being overheard, Molly told her.

Laura glanced sideways toward Fiona, now sipping tea with Aileen Morrison, Cameron, and a couple they didn't know. "You're overthinking it, Molly," Laura whispered.

"Maybe." Still, Molly couldn't shake off her impressions.

While Charlie Kinnaird didn't closely resemble his mother, their faces shared a similar sadness. Comparing her measured hostility, though, to the disturbed look in Charlie's eyes that evening when The Piping Yoopers played, Molly wondered if the young man was struggling more than his mom.

Laura tugged on Molly's arm. "Let's go outside. I think you could use some sunshine."

Of course her friend was right. The warm rays caressed her face and warmed her heart.

The day brightened further when Logan and Tanya Bruce invited Molly and her friends for a ride on their pontoon boat that afternoon.

"Logan's been aching to take it out since February." Tanya gazed at her burly, redheaded husband with amusement. "At least he waited until the snow melted off the sidewalks."

Logan, who had inherited his mother's broad smile and none of Hamish's grumpiness, shrugged amiably. "Don't let her fool you," he told the Bakehouse Three. "She enjoys it as much as I do."

There was no question that the couple's daughters loved the boat. Dressed in their Sunday best, they chittered and flew around like a flock of little birds at mention of the pontoon.

"Come with us." Leah tugged on Molly's hand. "Please?"

The partners and Harvey barely had to confer before accepting.

"We'll gladly serve as an excuse for your first ride of the year," Molly said. Skimming over azure water with this happy, boisterous family on a sunny day—it was the perfect cure for winter doldrums.

When Molly, Laura, Carol, and Harvey joined the younger Bruces at Logan's Mighty Scot Marina, Molly couldn't help but notice that the breeze, which had been so gentle in town, blew briskly off the water. Even more so as the pontoon rumbled across the lake.

But who cared? Winter had lost its grip. As they motored over the lake's deeper areas, through its mirror-like bays, and along picturesque shorelines, memories from her long-ago summers in Loch Mallaig played in Molly's mind like favorite movies. She'd loved those beautiful days when their group of friends had gone out on Fergus's sailboat. Fergus was a natural sailor but also a natural teacher, and she'd learned how to tack and jibe under his patient instruction.

"Earth to Molly," Laura crooned, then elbowed Carol. "I do believe she's thinking about Fergus."

"She does have that faraway look," Carol agreed. "And she hasn't stopped smiling since we left the dock."

"Fergus?" Seven-year-old Alannah had popped up between them. "I know Mr. Fergus. He's a nice man."

"Very nice." Laura fluttered her eyelashes at Molly.

The little girl eyed Molly as well. "Do you like him?"

Dismayed to feel a flush creeping across her face, Molly said, "We all like him very much." She pointed at a passing vessel at least four times the size of Logan's. "Oh my, what a big boat."

Alannah shrugged. "That's the mayor's boat. We see it all the time."

"It used to be Mayor Kinnaird's boat." Logan, bless him, tickled his daughter's neck so she giggled and ran to her mother. "Doug's pride and joy. Spent every spare minute he could on it."

"I can see why." An aura of luxury surrounded the yacht. Molly recalled Kinnaird's famous parties as chronicled by Jane Thomson. She could imagine music, lights strung around its large upper deck, revelers dancing a summer night away. "So Mrs. Kinnaird sold it?"

Logan grimaced, as if he couldn't imagine anyone wanting to sell the yacht. "She sold it to the owner of the Moose Lake Country Club within a few weeks of Doug's death. She never did take to boating the way he did."

"I'm glad my wife likes my boat." Harvey encircled Carol's shoulder with his arm. "Even if it's not quite as fancy as that."

"You think?" Carol teased as Molly and Laura grinned. Harvey swore that his old boat, with its cranky motor, attracted more fish than he could catch.

Logan cast a wistful glance at the yacht as it pulled away. "When Fiona started taking bids, I would have thrown in my hat, but Tanya was right. With four college educations looking us in the face before we know it? Nope."

Amid his monologue about the high prices of everything—maybe Logan did resemble Hamish in some ways—Molly pondered Fiona Kinnaird's quick sale. Would a truly grieving widow sell something so near and dear to her late husband's heart? Perhaps, if she needed money to live on. Instead, Fiona apparently had used the proceeds from its sale—or a considerable life insurance payout—to fund her year of traveling.

Later, they floated past the cottage the ex-mayor's wife was turning into a castle. From the water, the skeletal frames of additions on every side appeared even bigger than they had from shore the other day.

"Fiona didn't waste much time after she got back to town, did she?" Carol mused, and her partners murmured assent.

Once the house was out of sight, the women made a silent agreement to shelve thoughts of the Kinnairds and spend the beautiful day on happier subjects. Molly enjoyed discussing birds along the shore with the Bruce girls. Thanks to their grandfather, they'd become experts, pointing out common loons, ducks, trumpeter swans, and even a pair of bald eagles soaring high in the cloudless, china-blue sky above the boat.

Spent drinking in the lake's beauty, playing with the girls, and chatting with friendly, down-to-earth Tanya, the afternoon passed quickly for Molly, and soon it was time to head back. As they chugged toward the marina, she spotted a stooped figure on the main pier.

Logan grimaced. "It's Vernon. Wonder what good news he has for me today."

"He's just a lonely old fella," Tanya countered. "Wave at Mr. Pennycook, girls."

The white-haired man acknowledged their attentions with a meaty hand, then assisted Logan with docking and tying up the boat. Carol and Harvey, whose legs were longer than Molly's and Laura's, stepped onto the dock and helped Tanya and the girls cross the narrow strip of water between boat and pier.

Laura managed to leap across, but Molly eyed the cold water and balked. "Guess I need help too."

"At your service, ma'am." Harvey extended his hand with a gallant flourish.

Logan introduced them to Vernon Pennycook as the owner of The Auld Crabbit, a bait shop with an apartment upstairs where he lived, but the old man barely acknowledged them. He had one thing in mind, and one only. "Lad, you best be staying around and keepin' an eye on your marina," he told Logan. "There be bad boats abroad on the lake these past few nights."

Bad boats? What does that mean? Molly exchanged glances with her partners.

Tanya's smile tightened, and she hurried her children toward the marina's buildings.

Logan, however, had recovered his easy manner. "Thanks, Vernon. I appreciate your keeping an eye on things."

Consternation creased the older man's already weathered face. "And I'll keep watchin' every night. How long until the police do something about those hooligans?"

Logan listened patiently as Vernon ranted. His grumblings quieted somewhat, however, when Logan invited him to share in the Scottish sticky toffee pudding Tanya had brought.

"Aye, that'd be a bonny treat." Vernon accompanied them to the marina's snack bar. Although a sign on the door indicated that the building was technically still closed for the season, Tanya had unlocked it and plugged in the microwave so she could warm the dessert. The indescribable fragrance of the moist cake with its rich sauce greeted their noses as they entered.

"It's my family's recipe," Tanya said as they all dug into the scrumptious pudding, "handed down from my great-great-grandmother in Scotland."

"Perfect ending to a day on the lake." Logan gave his wife a peck on the cheek and served himself a second helping.

When Molly got up to toss her now empty paper bowl in the trash, a cluster of framed photos on the wall drew her attention. She ran her gaze over the images, each one depicting a grinning man—or occasionally a woman—holding a large fish. She identified the same blond, middle-aged man in several pictures.

"That's Kent Donner," Logan explained, apparently noticing Molly's interest. "Best fisherman in Loch Mallaig. He's the odds-on favorite in every competition we host, as long as he's in town."

"Och, but don't ye be forgettin' he wins with bait from my shop," Vernon put in, his voice emitting gruff pride. "A good lad, that Kent. Unlike that no-good . . ." The rest of Vernon's words were lost as he shuffled toward the door.

"Leaving, Vernon?" Tanya asked. "Can I send you home with a bit more pudding?"

"Nah, lass. One helping was enough." Vernon paused with his hand on the doorknob and again cautioned Logan about the threats prowling the lake at night. "Leave all yer lights on like I do, lad. Them that love the darkness hate the light."

As she buttoned her coat, Molly peered through the snack bar's large windows. She watched the old man hurry along the shoreline, the slight hobble in his gait not slowing him down at all.

"He'll walk the whole distance back to his shop, about two miles," Logan said, joining Molly at the window. "But in this nice weather, he'd be insulted if we offered him a ride."

"What was that about bad boats?" she asked, keeping her voice low.

Logan rolled his eyes. "Vernon's a bit territorial when it comes to the lake. Unless he's known a boat's owner for a decade, he assumes the guy's up to no good." He shook his head. "He probably scares away a lot of tourists. Sometimes I wonder how he keeps his shop open."

After saying thank you and giving goodbye hugs, Molly, Laura, and Carol headed for Laura's cozy and cheerful cottage to discuss how to organize their week while Harvey went home to let Angus out.

When they entered, Carol glanced around the white-walled living room, with its stone fireplace and pink, gray, and lavender accents. "Did we come to the wrong address?"

"You've done an amazing job with this room, Laura," Molly marveled. "And so quickly." She sank into a comfy armchair and couldn't help but wonder when she'd get to relax in her own space. "I can't tell you how special it has been to stay with you," she told Carol, "but it's funny how much I miss my dresser. And my favorite dishes."

"Of course you do." Carol patted her shoulder. "We all need our own space."

"It won't be long now, Molly." Laura smiled reassuringly. "We're all done with the painting. You'll be spending your first night there by midweek."

Picturing an evening by the bakehouse's big fireplace, drinking coffee from her favorite mug, Molly joined in the week's planning session with a lighter heart than she'd had in several days.

Before they finished for the night, though, she knew she should report on her meeting with Chief Thomson and her library findings.

"The chief's sifting through possibilities, but so far, no promising leads," she told her partners. "When I looked over the town's election laws, it appears that Calhoun's taking Kinnaird's place was on the level. However, when I reviewed the town council minutes again, names stood out during Kinnaird's last year—business people who went to the trouble of attending the meetings, some of them several times."

After she'd shared her list, Molly proposed they shift Monday morning's remodeling plans to the afternoon. During the first half of the day, they'd visit the shopkeepers who'd stood to lose the most if Kinnaird had succeeded in attracting a chain.

Laura winced. "With only two weeks before our grand opening, we're supposed to run around town playing detective? I'm a chef, not Sherlock Holmes."

"I'm not either." Molly tried not to imagine Chloe's reaction to her sleuthing. "And it's not like we don't have enough to do. But can we really focus on our business when we're still worrying about the break-in and the letter?"

"I'm sure the police will do everything they can," Carol said. "Still, we're the ones who signed the mortgage. No one will invest time and energy in resolving this like we will."

"I guess that makes sense, in a weird sort of way." Crossing her arms, Laura eyed her partners. "Okay, Sherlock I and Sherlock II, what do we do first?"

"Well, I've already shopped at Wee Bairns Clothing for my grandkids, so I've met Tillie Campbell," Carol said. "With her specializing in children's clothes, she would have taken a bad hit. Maybe I can get her to talk a little about it."

To Molly's surprise, Laura offered to drop by The Knit Hoose and feel out Aileen Morrison on the subject. "I've also been wanting to visit The Pied Paper. Helga Hofmeister's the owner, right? I love her scrapbook display." Laura grinned. "And I wouldn't mind buying a few things. For the bakehouse, of course."

"And I *desperately* need to visit Thistle and That," Molly deadpanned. "Why, if I buy birthday gifts for the next two years, I'll bet Doreen Giobsan will tell me everything I want to know."

Laura laughed. "I'll bet she will."

"Actually, I do need to visit the drugstore, so I'll sound out Cameron MacPhee." Molly tapped her fingers on the chair's arm. "I wish there was some way I could connect with the schools. Betty Anderson said Mayor Calhoun donates his entire salary to keep their technology up to date. I'd love to confirm that, but we don't have kids in the school system—"

"I signed up to volunteer in my grandkids' classroom. I bet I could find out," Carol offered.

"Great. I think that covers everything I've thought of—so far." Molly cocked her head. "How about you girls?"

Mischief gleamed in Laura's eyes. "If we ask Vernon Pennycook, I'm sure he'll tell us everything bad about everyone."

"And then some," Molly agreed. "Though I'm not sure he would. We're outsiders, remember? Even if we do know the Bruces."

"True," Carol said. "But I saw Harvey charming him with his extensive outdoor knowledge, and I know he's planning a few spring fishing purchases. Maybe that'll soften Vernon's opinion. If we decide to fish after dark this summer, hopefully he won't call the cops on us."

Molly chuckled and told them Logan's explanation of the "bad boats" the elderly man had warned about. "He said Vernon gets a little overzealous about the lake."

Laura hooted. "A little?"

Molly's mirth faded. "When I was here as a kid, nobody worried about bad anything. We swam and boated and ran around at night, and our parents never gave it a second thought. Vernon's probably paranoid, but you have to admit, times have changed. Even in Loch Mallaig."

Once again, Molly envisioned the blood-red slashes of paint near their bakehouse's back entrance. Even now, her palms grew clammy as she recalled reading the letter—and thought about the fact that they might be visiting murderers on Monday morning.

Times had changed, all right.

Definitely not for the better.

10

Is it too early for a Green River float?

Molly smiled as she peered through the front window of MacPhee's Family Drugstore and saw that the old-fashioned soda fountain she'd frequented in her youth was still installed against a side wall.

Molly's smile slipped when the drugstore's door opened to reveal a small figure whose parka hood hid half her face—but only half. It was Fiona Kinnaird, who appeared not to see Molly as she hurried away in the opposite direction.

Molly glanced at her phone. It was just before nine o'clock, when the drugstore was scheduled to open. Maybe Cameron, Fiona's childhood neighbor, had let her pick up a prescription or some other purchase early? Such a favor wasn't unusual, especially in a small town. On the other hand, had Fiona carried a paper bag containing her items?

Molly couldn't remember.

She started to turn her thoughts instead toward how she would approach Cameron MacPhee about Kinnaird's chain stores, but the moment Molly opened the heavy front door of the drugstore, she was transported forty years into the past.

The fragrance of summers long ago tickled her nose. The aroma of hot cashews in a roaster by the soda fountain triumphed over the pharmacy's musty medicine smells, just as it had years before. The silvery, polished surfaces where soda jerks had worked still mirrored the tin-patterned ceiling.

Molly approached the white marble counter and sat on a slightly shabby red vinyl stool. Strange how the temptation to twirl the stool tugged on her as much as ever. *Mom's in Iowa.* Molly grinned and shifted the stool from side to side, then spun a full rotation with glee.

"Hello again." Cameron MacPhee appeared from the back of the store just as she completed her turn. "It's Molly, right?"

"That's right," Molly said, impressed that he'd remembered her name from the day he stopped by the bakehouse to say hello.

A smile tugged at his mouth as he approached. "Feel free to spin as much as you want."

She grinned in response. "I've been wanting to do that ever since I came here as a kid." Molly realized the current owner strongly resembled the nice man who had served her family ice cream so long ago. Cameron must be his son.

"Can I get you something?" he asked.

She glanced at the menu on the wall, which listed both modern offerings, such as mochas and iced coffee, and drinks from Molly's youth. She saw what she wanted and smiled. "I'll have a Green River float, please."

"Coming right up."

As Molly meandered around the store, picking out hair care products and makeup, the drugstore owner deftly concocted the fizzy green treat.

Upon its completion, Molly made a beeline back to her stool. At first sip, the indulgence transported her back to childhood. She savored it slowly, letting the tart-sweet-creamy taste roll on her tongue.

She chatted with the druggist as he replenished fountain supplies, wondering how to introduce the subject of chain stores. No doubt that would end their pleasant conversation.

Molly decided to wait until she'd finished every drop of her float.

An elderly man wearing a huge, furry hat, entered the drugstore and strode to the soda fountain. "You're one of those new bakers who bought the Bailey place," he said to Molly. "Were you the one that found that letter?"

Cameron stiffened as he wiped down the counter.

"Well, yes," Molly answered hesitantly. "My partners and I—"

"I heard it said that Mayor Kinnaird didn't really die of a heart attack." The newcomer's beady eyes searched Molly's face as if trying to read her mind. "Maybe somebody wanted to get rid of him?"

"Of course he died of a heart attack," Cameron snapped, then instantly backtracked. "I'm sorry, Mr. Cordry. It's been a difficult week, but that's no excuse. How can I help you?"

Cameron sounded apologetic as he directed the elderly man to arthritis remedies, but fire burned in his eyes as he stocked straws and napkins. Molly decided not to mention chain stores. She finished her drink and left.

As she exited the drugstore, Molly nearly collided with Charlie Kinnaird. She took a few steps back and met his gaze. He glared as if hoping his stare would incinerate her.

Flustered to the point of speechlessness, she wrenched free of his scrutiny, pivoted on her heel, and walked away, not really caring what direction she took. After a block or two, she paused, breathing deeply, as if to expel some poisonous gas she'd inhaled.

She hadn't said a single word to Charlie. Why had he acted as if she were responsible for every problem in his life?

The sight of the church's steeple rising above the other buildings guided her to Highland Street. She'd intended to talk to Reverend Findlay sometime anyway, and his friendly face and reassuring faith would be a welcome change after her uncomfortable encounters with Cameron and Charlie.

Spotting the pastor walking between the church and the parsonage, she called out a hello and waved—then realized he was wearing jeans. Monday was probably his day off.

Reverend Findlay paused and waved back. "Hello, Molly. Would you like to come in for a cup of tea?"

"Isn't it your day off? I don't want to impose."

"Not to worry," the pastor said. "Bonnie wouldn't forgive me if I let you get away without letting her play hostess."

Bonnie, Reverend Findlay's wife, welcomed Molly to Loch Mallaig and seated her in their cheerful breakfast nook, where conversation blossomed. Bonnie had attended college at Molly's alma mater, Newkirk College, several years before Molly and her partners. Their reminiscences of university life had the pastor looking heavenward, but he laughed with them as he shared a few of his own.

When the conversation shifted to Molly's move to Loch Mallaig and the opening of the bakehouse, Pastor Findlay asked, "Have the police made any progress in finding the burglar?"

Molly hadn't expected such a direct question, but she answered, "Not that I know of." She decided to be equally frank. "I've been doing my own research about Mayor Kinnaird. At first, it seemed very unlikely that anyone would want to get rid of him. Everyone seemed to love him. But now I'm not so sure."

"He had many friends and supporters." A hint of shrewdness passed over the pastor's kind face. "But I've never known anyone who didn't have a few adversaries."

"True," Molly said. "I understand Mayor Kinnaird and our present mayor had major differences of opinion."

"Both were stubborn Scots, and they argued all the time." Bonnie laughed.

"They were at opposing ends of the political pole," Reverend

Findlay agreed. "Still, they managed for years to attend town meetings without throwing punches at each other."

"There's something to be said for that." Molly debated whether to dig further, then plunged in. "Mayor Kinnaird's death must have been difficult, not only for the town, but for his family."

Bonnie stirred her tea. "It's been hard for the town to recover, but we're on our way, I think."

"And Kinnaird's wife and son?" Molly pressed.

"I pray they're beginning to heal," Reverend Findlay said quietly.

Sensing a shift in the room's energy, Molly drained her cup and stood. "Thanks so much for the tea and for letting me interrupt your morning."

"Always glad to get to know a new friend." Bonnie, beaming again, clasped her hand.

"Come by again soon, and bring your partners," Reverend Findlay urged. "And best believe we'll be visiting your bakery when it's open. Often, if Bonnie will let me."

"Only as often as we can without having to buy bigger clothes," Bonnie said with a smile.

After Molly left, she didn't quite know what to think of the visit. On one hand, she'd been welcomed with open arms. On the other, both the reverend and his wife had swiftly deflected any inquiries about Fiona and Charlie Kinnaird. *Not surprising, of course. A good pastor keeps parishioner confidences.* Perhaps she shouldn't have asked about them at all.

Distracted and feeling awkward, she took a wrong turn from the church and ended up walking farther from Bread on Arrival than closer to it. She was getting used to navigating Loch Mallaig's often charmingly curved or angled streets, so she knew that she'd eventually wind her way back to the bakehouse with enough left turns. When she reached Loch Ness Lane, however, she spotted Between the Pines Bookshop and decided to nose around a little. Sure, Grizela had piled half a dozen tomes on her of which she had yet to read even the titles, but she simply couldn't resist a bookstore.

The log cottage was nestled, as its name declared, between two tall white pines. As she stepped inside its barn door, the owner greeted her. It was Grizela's nemesis, the ponytailed man. "Well, hello," he said. "Again."

He clearly remembered Molly from the library, and the awkwardness she'd felt upon leaving the Findlays' returned.

"I'm John Buchanan." He held out his hand. "You're new in town, aren't you?"

"Molly Ferris," she said, shaking his hand.

"Ah yes, one of the intrepid entrepreneurs reimagining the old Bailey place as a bakery." His tone was more encouraging than teasing, and fortunately he didn't bring up the burglary or the letter about Mayor Kinnaird. Instead, he gave her a mini tour of his quiet shop, then said, "Feel free to browse as long as you like, and let me know if you have any questions."

"Thanks a lot." Molly wandered the aisles but soon realized she probably wouldn't find a book that suited her tastes. Most of the books focused on Eastern thought, Native American mysticism, and holistic medicine.

Still, John had been kind, and she certainly wanted to encourage local business, so she took several pressed-leaf bookmarks to the cash register. "You have a unique shop," she said as he rang them up.

"It is. I'm glad tourist season's almost here. My sales—and yours—will shoot up fifty percent."

With that as a segue, Molly decided to mention to John what she'd wanted to discuss with Cameron earlier. "I heard something about a big discount chain coming to Loch Mallaig."

He shrugged. "That rumor surfaces every couple of years. I've lived here about twenty years. So far, it hasn't happened. Besides"—he flashed a smile—"most discount stores don't feature books like mine."

"Quite true." Molly paid for her purchases and left. Checking the time, she saw that it was much later than she'd realized. *If I'm going to move in anytime this week, I'd better get back to work.*

But as she passed Thistle and That, the gift shop next to the bakehouse, she remembered that she'd told her partners she would stop by. Hopefully she could do it quickly.

"Well it's about time you made it here," Doreen said cheerfully in greeting. "Did that old slave driver finally let you out?"

Molly grinned. "Hamish might be a little on the compulsive side—"

"A little?" Doreen sniffed. "I had him for history in high school. He worked us harder than all the rest of the teachers put together. I can still tell you every detail about Ferdinand Magellan's trip around the world in 1519—not that it does me any good here." She swept a hand toward her colorful, enticing displays. "Forget about Hamish and Ferdinand. Are you looking for anything specific?"

Molly checked her mental calendar, then said, "Actually, my mother's birthday is coming up. I'm sure you've got something she'll love here."

And indeed Doreen did. She helped Molly select a lovely china teapot, cups, and tray decorated with delicate pink roses. The purchase, as predicted, loosened Doreen's ready tongue. When Molly mentioned Fiona's remodeling project, Doreen knew plenty of details—or at least that was the impression Molly got from her arched eyebrows.

"Such a shame about Mayor Kinnaird, really," Doreen said as she deftly wrapped the teapot in tissue. "He was a great guy, even if I didn't agree with his big dreams for mega-commerce in Loch Mallaig." She continued talking without letting Molly get a word in edgewise. "And if someone murdered him? Well, that just doesn't happen here."

I hope the police find the guy and put him in jail for a million years."

The arrival of another customer brought an end to Doreen's chatter, and Molly hurried back to Bread on Arrival with her purchase. On the sidewalk, she met up with Carol, who also carried several shopping bags.

"Did you buy out Wee Bairns?" Molly chuckled.

"I was inspired by my first time volunteering in Maisie and Gavin's class this morning." Carol eyed Molly's large bag and shook her head. "This detective thing is going to break us."

"Think of it as contributing to the local economy, of which our bakehouse is now part." Molly mounted the steps and opened the front door, hoping Hamish had gone home for lunch. After being gone all morning, she really didn't want to face his critical glare.

Given Carol's expression, she must have been thinking similarly. They piled their bags in the main room and slowly headed upstairs.

When Molly entered the kitchenette, she rubbed her eyes. The cluttered, messy space had been cleared and scrubbed. The sparkling window gathered bouquets of sunbeams.

Laura popped her auburn head around the corner. "Doesn't it look beautiful? Joyce and Hamish did it."

The Bruces appeared from behind Laura. "Now, now," Hamish said modestly, "it's just a little moving-in gift, after all."

"Little?" By now, Molly had peeked into her bedroom and bath. "You've cleared away all the renovation clutter—and my apartment's probably cleaner than it ever will be again." She threw her arms around her thoughtful new friends. "Why, I could move my furniture in this minute."

"Well, maybe not this minute." Joyce held up her big picnic basket. "How about lunch first?"

And what a lunch it was. Thick ham sandwiches on Joyce's homemade, whole wheat bread were accompanied by crisp veggies and juicy strawberries. And for dessert, she'd brought apple hand pies, as plump and sweet as their baker. Molly hadn't realized how hungry she'd grown. And after poking and prying all morning, a relaxing time with friends hit the spot.

Joyce had to leave for an appointment and Hamish inhaled his lunch before returning to work, but the Bakehouse Three dined at a normal pace. As they ate, they reported on their respective retail reconnaissance missions that morning. Carol went first, telling them about her visit to Wee Bairns. Her nose crinkled as she spread more Dijon mustard on her sandwich. "I didn't expect Tillie Campbell to blow up when I mentioned Kinnaird. I almost had to talk her into selling me the clothes I wanted."

Molly helped herself to another strawberry. "What did she say?"

Carol grimaced. "She called him a sneak and ranted about how Kinnaird wanted to put her out of business."

"When you were volunteering at the school, did you find out if Calhoun donates his salary for computers?" Laura asked.

"As a matter of fact, he does," Carol confirmed. "The administration and staff are actually putting together a special day to thank him. He's contributed thousands of dollars for technology since he entered office. The party's their idea, not his, according to the school secretary. She said they may have to drag him to the celebration."

That sounded very different from the reaction that publicity-seeking Mayor Kinnaird might have had, Molly thought. Also, Calhoun's act of charity didn't characterize a murderer.

Unless he used it to blind the town to what he'd done.

Laura's report steered Molly back to other possibilities. Her partner had accumulated purchases of beautiful variegated yarn at The Knit Hoose and a gift for her aunt at The Pied Paper. "All on sale," she enthused. "Who needs chain stores?"

"Did you happen to find time amid your bargain hunting to feel out Aileen or Helga about Kinnaird?" Carol asked, eyebrow raised.

"Both shopkeepers seemed to think Kinnaird's proposals were reasonable," Laura said. "Helga wasn't upset at all. She said that if a chain store had moved in on her business, she wouldn't have minded retiring and finding something else fun to do."

Molly chose a hand pie and put it on her plate. "What about Aileen?"

"It seems that she didn't care for Kinnaird's big-city approach, but she considered him a good mayor overall," Laura answered. "She just wanted him to understand a small business owner's perspective."

Carol nudged Molly with her shoulder. "Did you find out anything?"

"Yes." Molly clucked her tongue. "Maybe helpful. Maybe not." She told them how Doreen and John had proved as even-keeled as Aileen and Helga. "But Reverend and Mrs. Findlay noticeably avoided commenting about the Kinnaird family, which makes me think at least some of Wilma's gossip was true."

Then Molly told them about Cameron MacPhee's transformation from helpful to hostile at Mr. Cordry's mention of the letter. "That, along with his rather vocal contributions to all the town council meetings during Kinnaird's last year, puts him on my suspect list."

The others nodded.

"Oh, and I saw Fiona Kinnaird leaving the drugstore just before opening time," Molly said. "She didn't see me, though. I also ran into Charlie Kinnaird. Almost literally." Hesitantly, she described the incident.

Laura stared. "What's his problem?"

"He doesn't even know you," Carol said.

"Assuming even twentysomethings are plugged into the Loch Mallaig gossip network, I imagine he identifies me with the letter and his father's death. If he's still grieving, he probably blames us for stirring up all that hurt again." Molly tapped her fingers on her knee. "Perhaps he's figured out that we've heard rumors about his bad relationship with his dad. That if the mayor was indeed murdered, Charlie's a top suspect."

"Charlie's had a hard year or two." Hamish, who had reappeared in the doorway, practically growled the words. His expression was stormy, and he glared at the three women angrily. "He doesn't need anyone else to make it worse. Why don't you leave the boy alone?"

With that, he stomped back down the stairs.

11

So far, "Mind the door, lad," and "Take it a little to the left" were the only words Molly had heard from Hamish as he helped Fergus maneuver her furniture into its new home.

That morning, she, Carol, and Laura had laid moneyless bets as to whether he'd show up, given his semi-blowup at lunch the day before. Both Laura and Molly voted no, and Carol alone had said he would. "Hamish is a man of his word. He'd only break it if he sprained both ankles."

"Didn't you see how mad he was?" Laura had shaken her head. "If he comes, it's only because Joyce made him."

Whether forced or not, Hamish had appeared as promised, though much quieter than usual. Joyce was helping Tanya with sick children, so Hamish could have played hooky and gone bird-watching with no one the wiser. Instead, he, Fergus, Harvey, and the Three were making short work of moving Molly into the apartment.

"You really are trying to keep it simple, aren't you?" Fergus didn't mention the discrepancy, but Molly's worldly possessions hardly filled half a moving truck, whereas they'd needed a full truck and then some to move Laura's belongings into her cottage. Where her friend was doubling her living space from her former studio apartment—and had accumulated furnishings accordingly—Molly had focused on downsizing, and she'd taken the task seriously.

"That's right." She couldn't help noticing the arm muscles outlined by Fergus's gray thermal shirt as he deposited a big box in her walk-in closet. "I wanted a place I can clean in an hour. My free time will be spent playing, not keeping house."

"Wise, indeed." Fergus pulled a face. "Sometimes I fantasize about living in a tent."

"You?" Molly hooted. She'd been to Fergus's home on a summer visit decades earlier, when it had belonged to his grandfather. "Your house is enormous. And *Castle*glen has the perfect name."

"Okay, so I like my space." He grinned. "I didn't say how big a tent."

Chuckling, Molly glanced out the window. Hamish had made another trip to the moving truck. While the handyman was loading a dolly with boxes, she quickly recounted what had happened the day before at lunch when Hamish had overheard their conversation and flown off the handle. "Do you know why Hamish would have reacted like that?"

Fergus grimaced, then nodded. "When Charlie was a high school student, he didn't fit in. Nerdy. A fanatical chess player. Hamish took Charlie under his wing, and they were close for a while. They still keep in touch, as far as I know."

Yes, Molly could see Hamish championing a misfit. "Our friend's like a good loaf of bread, I guess. Crusty on the outside, soft inside."

At that moment, Hamish stuck his head through the door, startling her. Had he heard what she'd said—again?

If he had, Hamish made no sign of it. "Time for me to leave. Joyce will be home soon."

Brushing dust from her hands, Molly clasped his. "Thanks for everything you've done, Hamish. Without your help with this whole project, we'd be looking at opening months from now instead of days."

His flinty face softened. Maybe he'd forgiven her for suspecting Charlie.

Maybe.

"Tell Joyce not to cook tonight, okay?" Fergus told Hamish. "I'm throwing a housewarming party for these lovely ladies at six. Except it will be at Castleglen." He threw a mischievous glance at Molly and added grandly, "My *castle*."

A warm flush crept up Molly's face. "Oh my. But you've helped us so much al—"

"It will be my pleasure to welcome you all to King's Heid Pub tonight," Fergus continued in his faux-lordly tone.

"King's Heid? But we're a mess." Laura, who was good at eavesdropping, pushed back her stringy hair as she entered. "I'm not sure we can repair damages by six."

"Or even six tomorrow evening." Molly knew she looked the worst. Thank goodness the mirrors were still packed.

"Fear not," Fergus said. "I've reserved a room for our feast, one with a side door you can use without being observed. Required dress shall consist of sweatshirts and jeans."

"You've got a deal, mister." Carol's wide smile chased away the weary lines around her mouth.

At the prospect of a delicious, fun dinner, new energy flowed through Molly. Despite blank walls, the freshness of her new space inspired a spring feeling, one that promised sunny days ahead.

Pulling out her phone to take a few photos of the kitchenette, Molly realized she hadn't sent the first picture to her mother.

"We need to document this special day—the first in your apartment." Laura waved Molly to a spot with better lighting, shifting her phone to gain the best view.

"I look horrible." Molly cringed. "I'll break your phone."

"You couldn't look horrible if you tried. Besides, you're not supposed to look like a runway model on moving day." Laura gestured. "Shift a little to the right."

Knowing Laura would take the photos no matter what, Molly straightened her sweatshirt and brushed a lock of hair from her face. "Hold that gorgeous smile." Laura took several pictures. "That backsplash makes a wonderful background."

"Hamish did a great job." Molly instinctively ran her fingers over the blue-and-white mosaic pattern he'd so painstakingly installed.

"Carol, come over here," Laura beckoned. "Harvey, will you take our picture?"

"Of course," Harvey said, taking Laura's camera and snapping photos of the three women in the kitchenette.

"Is this the first one we've taken together since we bought this place?" Carol asked. "Have we been so busy that we haven't taken any pictures at all?"

"I've taken a few for our website, but with the remodeling mess, they wouldn't have made the best PR impression." Molly winced. "I forgot to send any to my parents. It's just as well, since my dad—and his bad back—would probably have shown up on our doorstep, ready to rebuild the place."

Laura shook her head. "I keep sending cottage photos to my family, but none of the bakehouse. What was I thinking?"

"Never too late to make memories—or to record them." Carol pulled out her own phone and took more quick pictures of Molly and the apartment, then headed toward the steps. "Come on, we want to show off the main floor too. It's photo op time."

"But we only have an hour," Molly protested. "We should shower before dinner."

"You heard what Fergus said." Carol started down the stairs. "I plan to wash up and run a comb through my hair. End of makeover."

"Me too, so you're not allowed to look perfect, even if *Fergus* will be there." Grinning wickedly, Laura tugged on Molly's arm.

Oh well.

A few minutes later, Molly was glad she gave in.

They darted into the kitchen first. Its crisp gray-and-white decor, accented with shiny light fixtures and glass tile backsplash, seemed staged for a photo shoot. Now almost complete, with stainless steel ovens, appliances, and prep tables that juxtaposed captivatingly with the golden hardwood underfoot, it seemed eager to be put to work.

"This really is a dream kitchen," Molly marveled. "I don't know if I've seen a prettier place to cook, not even in a magazine."

She and Carol took pictures while Laura flitted around, fussing with the appliances in her new domain. Eventually, she simply stood and inhaled, as if already breathing in the tantalizing fragrances of shortbread cookies, oatcakes, and Selkirk bannocks. "I can't wait another day. I'm going to unpack my kitchen stuff tomorrow."

They meandered into the main room, where Carol snapped more photographs. While the other two had spent considerable time helping to remodel the kitchen, Molly had worked mostly in this area. Now, as she surveyed how the scrubbed-clean fireplace and freshly painted woodwork accentuated the rich gleam of the refinished floors, she realized how much they'd accomplished. How much love she'd invested in her dream, now coming true.

Molly hugged herself. Soon the rustic tables and chairs they'd ordered would grace the room, filled with happy customers enjoying Bread on Arrival's delicious fare.

"It's a little late to shoot good pictures of the door," Carol announced, gesturing to the stained glass window built into the front door. She sighed and pocketed her phone. "Hopefully, the sun will shine tomorrow. I'll bring my good camera and find the right time to capture the light coming through."

"I'd love nice photos for our website," Molly said. "All these are fair game for media promotion, right?" She made a face. "Except for the awful ones of me."

Carol elbowed her. "You can't look awful when your smile is the result of a job well done and a dream coming true."

"You're right." Tears came to Molly's eyes at the truth in her friend's statement, but she blinked them back. "Okay, ladies. We'd better hurry or we won't even have time to comb our hair before six."

A few hours later, they all were seated in a casual yet gracious room populated with servers who hardly let them lift a finger.

"This is a busy woman's dream." Having finished the delicious dinner, Joyce leaned back in her chair with a sigh.

"I thought I was your dream, hen." Hamish seemed to have mellowed considerably.

"You could be." Joyce threw him a flirty glance. "If you cooked me steak smothered in caramelized mushrooms, then did the dishes."

Molly didn't realize how she'd craved this evening, eating a wonderful meal with good friends in comfortable surroundings. Not to mention the flamed sweetness of the bananas Foster they'd had for dessert.

Though mostly content, she harbored a glow of anticipation for the still-to-come satisfaction of sleeping under her own roof.

Carol, though, was trying to persuade her to stay another night or two at their house. "I know your bed's set up, but can you find anything in that mess?"

"Have you forgotten it used to be a funeral parlor?" Laura asked with a shudder.

"I think the cow wallpaper scared me more than anything," Molly joked. "Now that it's gone, I can sleep without fear."

Carol persisted. "Do you think it's wise to stay in that big old place all alone?"

"I'll be just fine, Mom." Molly rolled her eyes. What—after all that work, she wasn't supposed to live in her own apartment?

But Fergus didn't seem enthusiastic either. "Maybe you should wait until the police have more leads. You had a break-in, remember?"

Joyce took Molly's side, much to her relief. "This girl lived in Chicago for years. She can stay home by herself."

Molly beamed at her, then raised a glass to thank their host. "I'd like to propose a toast to Fergus. Thank you for this incredible evening and for your help. If you hadn't found this building for us, we wouldn't have had anything to celebrate tonight. Our dream wouldn't have even begun to come true."

The smile that lit his face hadn't aged one iota.

Molly tugged free of its magnetism and slipped out before she was drawn back into her sixteen-year-old self. Romance was a complication she certainly didn't need to add to her already chaotic new life as a bakery owner—or at least that was what she kept telling herself.

Pulling into the bakehouse's parking lot, Molly was glad she'd picked up Angus at Carol's on the way home—and that she'd left a light on in her apartment.

The Victorian mansion loomed before her. Its large, dark yard held a thousand shadows.

They probably should install more security lights, especially given the break-in.

Molly shook herself. She probably couldn't count the number of burglaries that had taken place in her Chicago neighborhood. Why let herself be spooked in tiny Loch Mallaig, Michigan?

Angus couldn't wait to get out of the car, and that helped. Barking his joy, he led the way to the porch and bounded inside as if he knew this was home.

She flipped on lights, appreciating the rejuvenated main room's fresh feel once more. Molly turned the front door's dead bolt, left a small light on downstairs that reflected softly in the stained glass window, and followed her Scottie to the apartment.

When she climbed into bed, the warmth of her downy white quilt felt like a welcome-home hug. Angus brought his favorite toy, Woolie the sheep, to her bedside with a wistful stare, and Molly decided to break the rules. She patted the space near her, and in a split second, both Angus and Woolie were snuggled beside her.

What rules? Molly chuckled wryly as she petted her dog in the darkness. Why did she pretend rules existed when it came to her Scottie? Angus would sleep wherever he wanted, as he always had.

Tonight, his furry presence helped her drift off into sleep.

Until multiple crashes ripped Molly and Angus from their deep slumber.

Barking furiously, Angus streaked for the landing door, which he pawed at despite the fact that it was closed tight. Molly grabbed a robe and her phone, then dashed after him.

With one hand, she tried to restrain him. With the other, she dialed 911 and reported the noise. "I don't know what happened, but please come to 18 Tattie Bogle Road right away."

"What, Bailey's?" The operator sounded confused.

Not Bailey's, she wanted to yell. *Bread on Arrival.* "Yes. Please come now."

Stuffing the phone into her robe pocket, Molly grabbed a broom, the closest thing she could find to a weapon. "Come on, Angus, let's go get 'em."

Before she had time to think, she unlocked and threw open the landing door. Angus shot down the stairs, his barks like bullets. Molly charged after him, flipping on lights as she ran.

At the bottom of the stairway, her knees melted, and she cried out for Angus to come back to her.

The front door's window, with its elegant stained glass design, lay in countless shards on the floor.

Large, reddish rocks lay amid the destruction.

They looked as if they'd been dipped in blood.

12

"What were you thinking, charging downstairs like some kind of bakery warrior?" Laura's eyes sparked as she threw her arms around Molly.

"What if that nut had met you on the stairs?" Carol demanded, hugging both.

Harvey, his salt-and-pepper hair standing on end, said nothing, but concern shone from his bleary eyes.

All the love felt good, even if Molly couldn't begin to answer the questions. "I don't know. I just had to do something."

"Hopefully there won't be a next time." Chief Thomson looked grim as he took notes. "But if there is, let the 'something' be locking yourself in the bathroom or closet."

Now that she was safely surrounded by friends and police, Molly's bravado cooled considerably. She sank to the floor, tears welling as she checked Angus's pads for cuts from the glass. None, thank goodness. He nosed her, whining, as she surveyed the fragments of the original window, probably installed during the early 1900s. "I loved the way the sun came through it." She was determined not to cry, but a rebellious tear ran down her cheek. "I know. We're insured. We can pay a stained glass artist to create another one. But this glass? It's irreplaceable."

"*You're* irreplaceable," Carol said firmly. "And if you think we're going to let you sleep here by yourself the rest of the night, you're even crazier than you were when you camped out on our dorm roof."

Harvey stared. "Why'd you do that?"

A giggle and a sob tangled in Molly's throat so she couldn't answer. Laura rolled her eyes. "Just because she could."

"I agree that you shouldn't be alone," Chief Thomson put in.

"She'll stay with us," Carol told him.

Still coughing, Molly wanted to protest. Let this cretin scare her out of living in her own apartment? No way.

The chief fixed the Bakehouse Three with a worried gaze. "I heard about your little shopping trips around town, asking questions about Mayor Kinnaird's death."

Molly exchanged sheepish glances with her partners. Had they been that obvious?

He pointed to the mess on the floor. "I imagine the guy who did this heard about it too and wasn't exactly happy about it."

A small surge of triumph overrode Molly's embarrassment. The creep obviously felt threatened, which meant they might have made more progress than they thought in solving the mystery of the letter.

"I'd like to think this and the break-in were just the product of some slightly loony local who doesn't like nosy newcomers," the chief continued. "But if this has something to do with that letter and Kinnaird himself, this is more than just an expensive prank. It's a warning."

That word felt like an anvil falling on the room, and they all fell quiet.

Carol broke the silence in a calm tone. "We'll be careful."

Thomson shifted a razor stare from person to person. "I hope so. It's normal to want immediate results in an investigation, but these things take time. Do yourselves a favor and let the police take care of this."

They nodded silently.

"I'll have a squad car cruise the area several times each night for the rest of the week," the chief promised. "Let me know if you hear or see anything unusual, night or day, no matter how small it seems."

After a final check, he gave them permission to clean up the glass. Together, they hauled a large piece of plywood from the back porch to the main room, where Molly and Laura held it in place on the door while Harvey nailed it over the gaping window.

Though Molly thanked him profusely for helping ensure her safety, she fought tears again at the ugly sight, so different from its original beauty.

"Come on, Molly." Carol tugged on her elbow. "Let's go home. You too, Angus." She whistled for the Scottie, who usually ran to his next-best buddies without hesitation. This time, however, he sat on his haunches, cocking his head as if pretending not to understand.

"Here, boy," Harvey joined in.

"He doesn't want to leave." Molly straightened her spine. "And neither do I. Allow this *miscreant* to intimidate me?" She stuck out her chin. "Not going to happen."

Carol nailed her with her best strict teacher stare. "You're out of your mind."

"Maybe." Molly stuck her hands on her hips. "But that's the way it is."

Laura hadn't entered the debate, but now she sighed and said, "I knew you wouldn't budge. I brought a couple of sleeping bags."

A reluctant grin crept across Carol's face. "I did too," she admitted. "Plus air mattresses. If we're going to camp out, I'm not going to wreck my back doing it."

Laughing and shaking their heads, they hauled the sleeping bags inside and up the stairs. Another argument began when Molly insisted Carol and Harvey take the bed. Harvey protested that Molly and Laura should take the bed. Eventually, they decided to draw straws.

Angus, jumping onto the bed, made it clear that whoever chose it would share its comfy confines with him—and the winners were Carol and Harvey.

"I feel like I'm back at scout camp," Molly said. "Who feels like singing *Kumbaya* and toasting marshmallows?"

"Let's go to *sleep*, already." Laura, who had bedded down in the kitchenette, fluffed her pillow and plopped onto her sleeping bag, cushioned by the air mattress. "Turn off the lights before Chief Thomson drives by and realizes you're still here."

Molly snuggled deep into her bag. As she drifted off, a fragment of pity floated through her mind as she thought of their harasser. *Poor guy. I'll bet you don't have friends like mine.*

Early the next morning, as they dragged themselves out of their respective beds and decided on breakfast at Neeps and Tatties, Molly told the others she planned to invite Fergus.

"We may as well tell him our version of what happened," she said, "before he hears that faeries smashed our window and carried us off."

She pulled out her phone and texted him. *Want to come eat breakfast at Neeps and Tatties with us this morning?*

That will be quite convenient, Fergus answered, *as I was just about to knock on your busted front door. I'm guessing you have a story to tell.*

While they all hungrily dug in to full Scottish breakfasts of fried eggs, bacon, baked beans, tattie scones, and baked tomatoes, Molly summarized their night.

Fergus whistled. "I'm glad you had such great company. But I really think you should stay elsewhere until the police catch this guy. If it'll help, I'll stay in the apartment at night."

Carol jumped in before Molly could say a word. "That would be perfect. Molly can stay with us and be safe." She winced slightly. "Not that we want anything to happen to you, Fergus."

He chuckled. "I doubt I'd be taking much of a risk. Once word gets out that the police are patrolling your place—"

"Exactly," Molly interrupted. "With Wilma at the police station, the whole town will know before noon. If this burglar has half a brain, he won't attempt anything else—which is why I'm going to stay in the apartment. Why should you inconvenience yourself, Fergus?" Crossing her arms, she turned to her partners. "And you certainly don't have to camp out with me every night. It's my apartment. My problem."

"Here we go again." Carol rolled her eyes toward Harvey, who seemed to be choosing diplomatic silence in the matter.

"You've got that wrong, girlfriend." Laura matched Molly's glare. "We're partners, remember? This is *our* bakehouse. *Our* problem."

Rats. Having friends was wonderful—except when they were right. Molly exhaled. "All right. What do you think *we* should do?"

They brainstormed and bickered until Molly agreed to one of them staying a random two to three nights a week.

"Publicly, we'll act as if someone else is here with you every night," Carol said. "But when you're alone, Molly, if Angus lets out a peep—even if he's just chasing rabbits in his dreams—call one of us."

It wasn't really a question, but Molly answered, "Okay."

Obviously changing the subject to what he considered a happier one, Fergus asked Molly about the LaSalle. "Are you ready to learn how to drive a manual transmission? That sweet ride shouldn't stay hidden away forever."

Molly gave him a thumbs-up. "Sure I'm ready—though I'm not sure the LaSalle wants to lay down its life."

"It's not that hard," he insisted. "Not as easy as driving my golf cart or motorboat, but you'll catch on fast."

"You have a motorboat now?" Molly had thought he'd never go

for any boat that wasn't wind powered. "I mostly remember how much you liked your sailboat."

"I own a sailboat too, but waterskiing behind it wouldn't be much fun. Hey, you'll all have to come over and ski when it warms up." He brought up his phone's calendar. "Have any plans the first weekend in June? We'll call it a Welcome to Summer party."

"Sounds wonderful." Molly pictured a summer day like those long ago in Loch Mallaig. Waterskiing, sailing, swimming, the fragrance of fabulous food on the grill . . . but her reverie was interrupted by thoughts of all they needed to accomplish that day. She groaned and checked her watch. "Not to ruin the moment but—"

"Och, the mornin's wastin'!" Laura imitated Hamish too well.

"I'll bet he's already been hard at work for an hour," Carol said as they all put in money for their share of the bill and stood.

Molly really didn't need the curmudgeonly Scotsman berating them for lateness. She hustled into her coat and said goodbye to Fergus and Harvey, who both had work to do somewhere other than Bread on Arrival.

When they arrived, Hamish indeed was hammering away on shelves in the upstairs storeroom. Amazingly, he hardly gave them a second glance. Molly almost had to force a report about the front window on him.

He took nails from his mouth and nodded. "Yes, yes, I saw. I know all about that."

Fine. After all her friends' sympathy and concern, Hamish's indifference to the previous night's dangers raised Molly's hackles. Still, he hadn't launched into a tirade about their lateness, so she swallowed her annoyance and went downstairs.

She and the others joined forces to arrange boxes and bins in the kitchen. When their expected furniture delivery arrived, they tugged and pushed the new tables and chairs into place in the main room. The reality of the bakehouse's imminent grand opening lifted their weary spirits and eased the ache in their muscles and hearts as they tried to ignore the plywood window.

When their physical energy flagged, Laura began to research glass specialists in the Upper Peninsula. "We want that fixed as soon as possible."

While Laura made calls, Carol arranged for pickup and delivery of the antique counters they'd bought from Joyce's friend. She also checked the arrival date of a huge supply order they'd placed the previous week.

Molly reviewed their grand opening plans, updated the Bread on Arrival website and social media pages, then worked on a press release to send out to area newspapers.

"Looks like everything's on schedule—so far." Grinning, Carol knocked on a wooden cabinet.

"I really think we're going to make the target date." Molly beamed. "Less than two weeks from now, Bread on Arrival will be in business."

The others answered with high fives and hugs.

Hamish, standing on the stairway, grunted, then cleared his throat loud enough to be heard outside.

Their celebration halted as if he'd hit a pause button.

"I suppose I should stop fiddlin' around and say what I think," he said.

When have you ever not said what you think? Molly read the same sentiment in the others' faces. She readied her ears to ignore the lecture they'd been expecting all morning.

Instead, Hamish dropped a bomb. "I believe I know who wrote that letter and hid it in the cabinet."

13

As if rehearsed, their jaws dropped in sync.

"I think Grizela Duff wrote it." Hamish crossed his arms as if defying anyone to contradict him.

Molly finally found her tongue. "The librarian? Whatever would make you suspect her?"

"Would you doubt I have sufficient reason?" Hamish eyeballed Molly, then each of his other listeners.

No. Despite questioning Hamish's tact and general personality, none would ever distrust his sharp mind.

"Please tell us more," Molly said.

"It will take more than a minute, so I suppose we'll have to cease work for a bit." He sighed, then disappeared into the kitchen.

Molly, Carol, and Laura exchanged incredulous stares.

"And my New York friends thought living here would be boring," Laura said.

"I wish." Molly rubbed her temples. "At this point, nothing surprises me."

Hamish returned with a large basket. "When Joyce heard about the window, she sent her love." He added glumly, "And the muffins I thought were mine for breakfast."

After their huge Neeps and Tatties meal, Molly and her partners were still mostly stuffed, so they shared one muffin among themselves and left the lion's share for Hamish.

Mellowed by a carrot muffin, Hamish started by telling them

they must keep his revelation confidential until he decided what to do. "I'd hoped the truth would rise to the surface without me getting involved, but with a break-in and rock throwing and such, I can't keep my peace any longer."

They all nodded acquiescence. Between bites, Hamish began to explain that, for years, he'd often worked part-time for Jim and Hennie Bailey. Given Mayor Kinnaird's popularity, they'd pressed Hamish into service for his wake and funeral.

"I was in and out, carrying flowers and setting up chairs, when I saw Grizela sneak into the viewing room before calling hours." Disapproval colored his voice. "Wouldn't have expected it of her, but there it was."

For once, Molly didn't try to be patient. "Go on."

Hamish frowned, but continued. "I saw her put something into the coffin, something white." His forehead furrowed into a terrace of wrinkles as his voice rose. "She wasn't family, not even a distant relation. Where would the mayor be if everyone filled his casket with stuff? Not that he needed room to stretch his legs." Hamish paused for a chuckle and looked around for a similar response.

Molly didn't laugh. No one else did either.

He cleared his throat again. "I was about to confront Grizela when the front door buzzed. More flowers to be carried in. I'd never seen so many at one funeral. By the time I returned, Grizela was nowhere to be found. I searched the mayor's casket—respectfully, of course—but didn't find anything. Figured Grizela had had second thoughts, but she's never been one to change her mind. I've wondered about it ever since. Now, with finding this letter, I'm wondering more than ever. Why would she write a letter like that? Did she take it back from the casket and hide it in the cabinet?"

"If she did, why did she leave it there until now?" Carol wondered.

No one mentioned the break-in, but seeing her partners' expressions, Molly knew they were thinking the same thing she was: Knowing they might soon find the letter, had Grizela attempted to retrieve it? But would she have spray-painted the back entrance? Or thrown rocks through their window? Those juvenile tricks didn't seem to suit the stern librarian.

Hamish brushed muffin crumbs from his hands and straightened. "I expect it's time to stop fiddling around and ask her."

Hamish was right. But when Molly recalled Grizela's fiery encounter with John Buchanan, the thought of a head-on collision between her and their handyman was too scary to imagine.

"I'll go with you, Hamish," she heard herself say, then immediately grimaced.

"Do you think that's necessary?" Carol stared at Molly as if she'd lost her mind, as did Laura.

"Absolutely." Now that she'd said it, Molly knew she was right. "All this involves our bakehouse, doesn't it? I know Grizela best of the three of us, correct?"

Carol and Laura nodded reluctantly.

"But she has a reputation for being a dragon," Carol said. "Jenny once said Grizela breathes fire when you turn in books late, and she didn't look like she was kidding. Maybe I should go with you too."

"Me too." Laura raised her chin.

Molly shook her head. "We can't turn this into a vigilante committee. Besides, if she feels like we're ganging up on her, she might be too on her guard to tell us anything."

"Indeed." Hamish's quiet comment silenced them all. "Molly may go with me, but there's the end of it." He paused. "As for Grizela, I've known her for years. I respect all she's done for Loch Mallaig. While she shouldn't have been sneaking around the mayor's casket"—his teacher voice had taken over—"Grizela must believe she had good reasons for doing what she did. I want to hear them."

"As do I." Molly consulted her phone calendar. "When do you want to go?"

"The sooner the better. We'll go at lunchtime."

Molly blinked. Hamish was already headed toward the kitchen to resume whatever project he was working on at the moment.

Unfortunately, he was right again. If she didn't do this soon, she'd talk herself out of it.

Molly and the others threw themselves into cleaning every corner of the bakehouse. This afternoon, she'd begin to organize the office upstairs. With everything so crazy, it might be nice to exert control over something.

After they ate their brown-bag lunches, Molly figured she was as ready as she'd ever be.

Walking with Hamish toward the library, she wished like crazy she was just returning overdue books.

When they entered Grizela's domain, her eyes sparked at the sight of Hamish. "Didn't I tell you your bird book wouldn't be in until next Tuesday?"

"You did, indeed," he answered. "We needed to consult you on another matter."

Hamish certainly sounded more polite than usual. Molly glanced at her companion. Could their crusty handyman be dreading this encounter as much as she?

"What book are you looking for?" Grizela cocked her head.

"Er, not a book."

"A magazine? A newspaper?"

Another patron approached the circulation desk, and Hamish deferred to him. Grizela answered the man's question with her usual efficiency, sending him to the library's extensive genealogy area. She turned back to Hamish and Molly. "Now, what can I do for you?"

The phone rang, and Grizela answered it, then rattled off some helpful information. After hanging up, she dropped her hands. "A busy day. What did you need?"

"We don't need anything but a minute of your time." A note of impatience had finally crept into Hamish's voice. "Preferably in your office."

"Well, don't fuss. I've got a minute, anyway." Grizela gestured toward her closet-like space. As Grizela closed the door, Molly noted the impeccable organization around the ancient computer.

The librarian sat straight as a general. "Tell me what's on your mind."

No longer bothering with diplomacy, Hamish shot straight from the hip. "I saw you put something in Mayor Kinnaird's casket. We want to know what. And why."

Grizela's face turned to stone.

Molly held her breath.

No one uttered a sound for what seemed an eternity.

At last, Grizela said, "I had my reasons."

"I know you did. And we need you to tell them." Hamish gestured toward Molly. "This lady and her partners already have endured much because of the letter they found. Did you write it and hide it in the cabinet?"

Grizela glanced past him through her windowed door. "'Tis not the time nor place to consider such questions."

Hamish didn't budge. "I think it is."

"That is because this is not your workplace." A little of Grizela's usual vinegar flavored her retort. "I see two patrons standing at my desk and another approaching. If you want to talk with me, please come to my house tonight. Six o'clock, before my historical society meeting."

"Very well." Hamish stood and exited.

So much for Molly's participation. The only word she contributed to the entire effort was a rather weak goodbye as she trailed after Hamish.

With little to report to the others afterward, Molly tried to keep her mind on setting up the bakehouse's new office computer.

A few hours later, she decided even Hamish couldn't out-cranky the confounding machine. Unlike humans, though, she could power this one down.

She needed a break. Molly walked downstairs to touch base with the others, Angus following behind her. At the landing, however, he slipped ahead of Molly and ran.

"Angus, come back here. Angus!"

Unfortunately, she knew where she'd find him. Angus had developed an inexplicable liking for Hamish.

Her handyman had been installing cabinets behind the new sales counters. He'd paused, however, to emit a disapproving harrumph.

Angus sat as close to Hamish as he could, wearing a doggy smile as big as Molly had ever seen. His tail whipped back and forth over the floor as he gazed up at the grumpy handyman with open adoration.

"I'm sorry." She picked up her Scottie. "He's faster than I am."

Hamish didn't comment further. There was no need to. His expression said it all.

Molly hauled her pet upstairs. "Angus, you usually sense whether people like dogs. Hamish obviously doesn't. Why haven't you figured that out?"

Angus just panted happily at her.

Molly closed the landing door, then spent the rest of the

afternoon organizing her desk and arranging the cute office accessories she'd bought.

And wondering. Wondering what Grizela would tell them in two hours . . . one hour . . . after Molly's hasty bowl-of-cereal supper. Hamish reappeared at the bakehouse's front door at quarter to six on the dot. Still in grunt mode, he said little as they walked to Grizela's house, which wasn't far from the library. A prim, pretty 1940s bungalow, it presented a tidy contrast to the somewhat shabby house next door.

Molly didn't dwell long on the curb appeal gap because Grizela answered the door before Hamish knocked. Delicious scents wafted through the house as the librarian seated her guests in the parlor, each with the obligatory cup of tea. A bit grudgingly, Grizela offered a hand-painted plate of shortbread she'd obviously baked for her meeting.

Even that gesture didn't mellow Hamish. "Now, Grizela, we're waiting. What did you put in the mayor's coffin?"

She met his gaze, unblinking. "You must talk to Vernon Pennycook."

Molly wilted. This was her explanation?

"Did Vernon write the letter?" Hamish demanded.

"Ask him yourself." Grizela's face darkened, except for the sparks that flew from her eyes. "He will tell you John Buchanan is behind all that's evil in Loch Mallaig."

The owner of Between the Pines? Molly recalled his politeness during her visit to his shop. What could Grizela mean?

Hamish issued rants and demands to no avail. Grizela sipped tea, ate most of the shortbread, and refused to say any more.

Molly finally edged Hamish out the door. He continued to fume as they walked home. "She could have told us that in three minutes at the library," he muttered. "Must have had second thoughts. Didn't want a finger pointed in her direction, no doubt."

"What do you think she meant by pointing one at John Buchanan?"

This time, Hamish's harrumph held a note of amusement. "Those are two neighbors who wouldn't get along in heaven."

"John lives next door?"

"In that slovenly heap? Yes. Ever since he moved from Nova Scotia about twenty years ago."

"But his shop is organized, and the outside is well maintained."

"True, though I think he hires A+ Scotland Yard for that," Hamish said, and Molly recognized the name of the lawn service they'd contracted to care for the bakehouse's exterior. "I wouldn't be surprised if John neglects his house strictly to annoy Grizela. She blathers on about his lack of upkeep, about the weeds that invade her lawn, and the way he lets his cats run loose."

Molly suppressed a smirk, thinking about the Bruces' manicured landscaping. I'll bet you wouldn't be thrilled by any of that either.

Hamish continued, "John rents a room to a guy named Kent Donner, a commercial fisherman who's gone a lot of the time. Kent keeps it tidy when he's at home, and Grizela loves him for it."

Molly nodded, recognizing the man's name. "I saw photos of him on the wall at the marina snack bar. And Vernon had nice things to say about him."

Hamish chuckled. "That's a rarity, indeed."

"Vernon clearly doesn't feel the same about John Buchanan. He and Grizela have that in common."

"That they do. She's tattled to the town council about the weeds countless times and called animal control about the cats. She even told John to his face his books are of the devil."

Molly blinked. "How did he respond?"

"Agreed with her. Couldn't have done anything that would have made her madder." Hamish cocked an eyebrow at Molly. "Bet you're wondering why neither has moved away in all these years. Well, Grizela has lived in that house since she was sixteen, and she's not about to be run out of it by some outsider. And that's likely to be Vernon's problem with him as well."

"Outsider?" If John was still considered one after two decades, how long before Molly and her partners rated the town's acceptance? Hamish seemed to read her mind. "Some people just don't click. Some, like Kent, who moved here maybe five or six years ago, fit in right away." He paused, and a sly smile crept across his lips. "You and your friends, now—we might be willing to issue you birth certificates."

She warmed to the first compliment he'd given them but said, "Sounds like John stays in his house just to annoy her."

"How true." His mirth faded. "I'd usually vouch for Grizela's word any day of the year. She's a canny one. But in this case, I'm in no hurry to point a finger at John—even if he's a soft one that's always lived off his mother's money, even before she died."

That made sense, considering his store's obscure inventory.

What didn't make sense was Grizela's directive that they talk to Vernon Pennycook. Given Logan Bruce's comments about the old man's paranoia, would talking to him improve on Grizela's prejudice? Even if he admitted to writing the letter, there was no guarantee they'd get anything helpful out of him.

Nevertheless, the next afternoon, Molly found herself walking with Hamish along Dumfries Park's blustery shoreline to The Auld Crabbit.

Would Vernon regale them with wild tales of hooligans that existed only in his mind?

Or had the old fisherman hooked a real clue, one that would explain what was actually going on?

14

As Molly and Hamish approached the bait shop, which was as old and weather-beaten as its owner, she felt Vernon's probing stare from the doorway.

No hellos were exchanged. Instead, Vernon and Hamish greeted each other with brotherly insults.

"You." Vernon scowled. "What're you doing here? I don't need any more bad 'uns hanging around my store."

"I'll be gone in a wee minute." Hamish glared at him. "Why would I waste time with a *bampot* such as you?" Apparently his use of Scottish words increased, along with his brogue, when he was around another Loch Mallaig resident with the same verbal habits.

"Um, hi, Mr. Pennycook." Molly didn't know what else to say.

He squinted. "Do I know you, lass?"

Lass? Certainly not an insult in her book. However, since they'd met only days before, Molly's confidence in Vernon fell a few notches.

Hamish cut to the chase. "Grizela says you might know something about the evil in Loch Mallaig these days."

"That I do." Vernon's face creased further, adding even more wrinkles. "Bad boats abroad on the waters at night. Bad men trying to hide their sins." His hazel eyes glinted. "But they don't hide from me."

Molly barely restrained a sigh. What did this have to do with the letter?

"Grizela said John Buchanan is behind it all," Hamish said brusquely. "Why?"

"Because I saw him, sure as death, standin' in the dark by the lake two nights ago. Down at the other end of town. Recognized him by that ugly leather coat of his. Not the first time either."

Molly paused. At least Vernon seemed to base this opinion on tangible events. However, she couldn't consider an eyewitness account by Vernon "sure as death." Besides, why should John's presence by the lake at night incriminate him? Perhaps he was an insomniac and walking helped him sleep.

Hamish pushed on. "What time?"

"I don't know," Vernon snapped. "In the wee hours, when all decent men should be in their beds—exceptin' those who are keepin' watch over the town. That Buchanan met one of them bad boats there."

When Vernon veered off on a rant against the general evils of the times, to which Hamish interjected occasional, enthusiastic agreement, Molly pondered the fisherman's report. In Vernon's mind, the "wee hours" could have meant any time after nine p.m. The "bad boat" could have been manned by friends, offering John a fish or two from a productive night on the lake.

Right now, in a competition between Grizela and Vernon for least objective viewpoint, Molly wouldn't be able to decide.

Finally, Hamish steered the conversation back to John Buchanan. "Vernon, was that the only night you saw the bookseller and the boats?"

"Naw. Saw him with one last November as well."

Five months ago? Molly didn't roll her eyes, but the restraint took considerable effort. She decided to cut to the chase. "Would John have anything to do with the letter we found?"

She didn't bother to explain, certain Vernon knew about it.

Sure enough, he nodded. "Yep. I'm thinkin' he does."

"Did you write that letter, Mr. Pennycook?" Molly asked.

He raised his head like an indignant gull. "Why would I do that? If I've something to say, I say it."

Well, that was certainly true. While the two old men discussed the aches and pains of various relatives, along with their own, Molly tried to make sense of the whole scenario.

Finally, with a few more parting insults, they said their goodbyes. Vernon, however, issued a final warning to Molly. "Stay away from that bookseller, lassie. There's nothing to be gained by keeping bad company."

Molly held her peace as they walked a block or two toward the bakehouse. Then she said tartly, "I haven't the faintest idea why Grizela would want us to talk to him. Or why we should listen to either of them."

"*Wheesht*, Molly." Hamish's soothing voice only raised her hackles further. "I have known Vernon and Grizela since we were young. Both my friends have true hearts. They recognize evil when it's present. That's a rare thing these days."

"Do you still believe Grizela wrote that letter?"

"After considering it a while, yes. If not, she would have outright denied it." Hamish gave her his teacher look. "If both her and Vernon think John Buchanan is up to no good, then I'm thinking it may be true."

Annoyed beyond speech, Molly failed to notice a crack in the sidewalk and stumbled.

He caught her arm. "I know you want to know the truth about all this, as do I. But take Vernon's advice. Stay away from John Buchanan. At least until we decide our next move."

Until we *decide*? A defiant Molly waited on the bakehouse's front sidewalk until Hamish had driven out of sight. She whirled on her heels, then headed down Tattie Bogle Road toward Loch Ness Lane—and Between the Pines.

As she entered John Buchanan's domain, beams from the

late-afternoon sun lit its interior and streaked the owner's blond ponytail. His warm greeting held a faint note of surprise. "Back so soon?"

"I was in a bit of a hurry last time," Molly hedged. "I have a few more minutes now."

"Make yourself at home. Would you like a cup of coffee? We have one of those pod doohickeys for customers in the back corner."

"I'm okay, but thank you." Molly took a leisurely stroll around the shop, this time noticing a few more books that were to her liking. She chose one about the area's history to buy and took it to the register.

Ringing it up, John observed, "Guess this was a pretty grim place at one time."

"I think you're right." Molly glanced at the book's cover, which featured a collage of sepia-toned pictures of burly miners, fur-dressed traders, and armed Native Americans. "You'd never know it now."

"Loch Mallaig's a nice little town." He smiled as he bagged her purchase. "Occasionally, though, I need a change of scenery." His brown eyes brightened. "Last fall, I went to the Far East for a month. An incredible trip—be sure to visit Hong Kong if you ever get a chance. This year I'm headed to India in November. I'll be gone until Thanksgiving."

Listening to John enthusiastically share his plans, Molly marveled at his travels—and the fact he could afford the overseas airline tickets and boutique hotels he mentioned. *Your mother must have been a wealthy lady.*

"Do you close up your shop while you're gone?" Molly asked, wondering if the cold-weather slump in their tourist town was bad enough for him to shut down for weeks at a time.

"I reduce hours and have a part-timer work the register," John answered. "It's the same guy who leases a room from me, so I give him a break in rent. He doesn't work his real job as much in the winter, so he keeps an eye on things here, and I can be gone for weeks without worrying."

"That's a good trade-off," Molly said.

"It is," John agreed. "Have you done much traveling yourself?"

While discussing her trips to Central and South America, Molly told herself she'd spent too much time lately with suspicious old people. Because of them, she had been reading far too much into a truly pleasant conversation.

That evening, Carol and Harvey hosted a soup supper for the bakehouse group, perfect for a night that had reverted to winter iciness.

Absorbing the warmth of Carol's corn chowder and bread fresh from one of Laura's bakehouse test batches, Molly's tense neck muscles relaxed—slightly.

Fergus yawned. "I'm way too full, but I just couldn't leave that chowder alone. The bread was delicious too, Laura. You should consider opening a bakery." He grinned.

Laura's eyes twinkled. "I'll think about it."

"A lovely meal." Hamish pushed back his empty bowl and wiped his white mustache with a plaid napkin. He eyed everyone at the table. "Now that we're hale and hearty, it's time to put together a plan. How will we keep watch on Buchanan's place?"

Joyce gazed heavenward, probably offering her usual prayer for her husband's silence.

Fergus issued a quizzical gaze at Molly.

She shrugged. Evidently, Hamish had made up his mind, hardening maybes into a rock-firm conviction of John Buchanan's guilt despite the lack of evidence.

"I didn't know *we'd* decided on anything, much less a stakeout," Molly said. They'd shared only a brief account of their visits with Grizela and Vernon before Carol called them to supper.

Now Hamish said, "Certainly, we decided." He carefully refolded his napkin. "Shall we schedule vigils for this weekend?"

Harvey gestured with a coffeepot. "Let's take this discussion into the living room where it's a bit more comfortable."

Everyone welcomed the suggestion, settling into overstuffed sofas and chairs around the fireplace—until Angus, thrilled that his dinnertime banishment was over, tried to nestle himself between the sofa and Hamish's feet.

The Scottie's adored "friend" stiffened.

Molly hurried the dog toward the kitchen, where she could corral him yet sit at the edge of the room and take part in the conversation.

Carol wasted no time making her feelings clear. "This Sunday is Easter. Besides, I'm not at all sure there's enough evidence to suspect John Buchanan of anything."

Laura nodded. "Lose a night's sleep just to count how many icicles fall off his roof? I don't think so."

Thanks, partners. Their agreement was restoring Molly's faith in sanity. Although she felt obligated to share what John had said about his expensive travel plans.

Laura whistled. "Wow, maybe we should sell books instead of baked goods."

"He lived off his mother even before she died and left him her money," Molly reminded her, then turned to Hamish. "Didn't he?"

"Aye." He shook his head. "He's told Grizela straight out more than once. Much to her consternation."

Having seen them clash, Molly thought John had probably enjoyed the librarian's outraged reaction. Something else occurred to her. "Joyce, did you ever meet John's mother? Did she come from Nova Scotia to Loch Mallaig to visit him?"

She could almost see Joyce scroll through her social files. "Last year, when we heard she died, we visited John to give our condolences. He said his mother's name was Diana. He was closing shop the next day and going back to Nova Scotia for her funeral." Now Joyce's smooth forehead crinkled. "No, I can't say I ever met Diana. He visited her occasionally, but she never came here."

"Most moms would visit, but maybe she just didn't like the UP." Molly shrugged. "Or they may have had a falling-out. But then, would she have continued to support his lifestyle?" Doubt surged through her. "She did support him, didn't she?"

Joyce's eyes sharpened. "He's always had plenty of money. But whether she supported him or not—"

"Maybe she didn't even exist," Hamish blurted.

Before he'd finished his sentence, Carol was typing words into a search engine on her phone. She announced, "No obituary for a Diana Buchanan last year in Nova Scotia. The only one I could find died back in 1998."

"Perhaps Diana had a different last name," Laura suggested. "If John's father passed away, she may have remarried."

"No," Joyce said flatly. "That same visit, John told us she was dead set against remarrying."

Nobody responded right away, and her words seemed to echo off the log walls.

Finally, Fergus turned to Hamish and Joyce. "Knowing Grizela and Vernon, I imagine they've already told the police their opinions."

"You imagine right," Joyce said. "Given her history with John and Vernon's, er, frequent calls, the chief probably hasn't given much weight to their information."

"So, if anyone is going to follow through with this lead," Fergus said, "it will be us."

Harvey, who had remained silent most of the evening, spoke up. "I see your point, Fergus. This whole thing has been making Carol crazy, and I want it resolved." He thumped the arm of his chair. "If you and Hamish are going to stake out Buchanan's shop, I'm in."

This is starting to sound like the neighborhood boys planning a backyard campout. Glancing at each man, though, Molly saw their determined faces. After all, they were discussing a possible murder. Could she blow off their concern even if she didn't share their conviction that John Buchanan had a thing to do with it?

Besides, all the troubling incidents involved her and her partners' bakehouse. How could they stand back when their friends were willing to inconvenience themselves to follow a lead—even a slim one?

Molly exhaled. "At this point, I don't know what to think. But if we're going to pursue this, better that we do it before the bakery opens. I'm in—as long as we keep Easter Sunday free."

After a beat, Laura and Carol chimed in, "Me too."

"I'm not." Joyce surprised them. "I never was any good at staying up at night."

"She isn't," Hamish declared. "She'd snore so loud she'd scare away our target, and then where would we be?"

Joyce fixed a scalding glare on her husband. "You might do better as a lookout, but as for snoring—well, you could compete with a rocket launch."

The Bruces' spirited banter continued, and the others couldn't help laughing and egging them on. Finally, Joyce coaxed Hamish to a draw by promising to cook breakfast for all who would lose sleep.

"That'll be more than a fair exchange." Smiling, Hamish patted his wife's shoulder. "Your breakfasts could make the angels sing."

With that, tensions eased and plans for the stakeout evolved quickly—until Hamish insisted on including Vernon and Grizela.

"No disrespect intended," Fergus said, "but Vernon calls the police if a fish jumps too high. We don't want to antagonize the chief."

"I'll keep Vernon with me." Hamish raised his chin. "We wouldn't have a lead at all, were it not for him. And Grizela."

No one could argue with that. But who would temper Grizela's hostility toward John?

Molly tried to evade Hamish's eyes, but he bolted his gaze to her. "Grizela likes you, Molly. I've heard that she plans to visit the bakehouse often because you're hardworking and pleasant to boot." With a sweeping gesture, he declared, "We all know you're the perfect one to—"

"Oh all right." Molly was in no mood to listen to his extended oratory, especially as, with everyone's eyes on her, she couldn't decline.

If only Hamish wasn't right so much of the time.

As they firmed up Friday and Saturday shifts and locations, however, Molly's sense of adventure returned.

When she and Fergus left—he and his sleeping bag were doing "guard duty" in the bakehouse's main room that evening—Molly said, "I know it's too much to expect, but how wonderful would it be if we could resolve all this uncertainty before the bakehouse opens?"

Fergus's mouth quirked in a grin, but his eyes were serious. "I know your business is first and foremost in your mind, Molly, but your safety is what really matters."

At the same time her pulse quickened with pleasure at his concern, her gut tightened. What dangers awaited them all as they tried to catch a possible killer?

Snuggling with Angus in her cozy bed helped allay a little of her angst. So did the knowledge that Fergus kept guard downstairs, alert to any new tactics their rock tosser might invent.

His reassuring presence, however, did not shut down Molly's brain. When her phone's display revealed that midnight had come and gone, Molly was still staring at the ceiling.

Exploring the answer to her question about John Buchanan's mother hadn't eased her mind one bit.

Instead, it had cracked open doors that she longed to shut.

15

The next morning, loud banging on the bakehouse's front door echoed through the building, as if someone were using a battering ram against the temporary plywood nailed in place of the window.

"What in the world?" Molly, opening newly arrived boxes of pans, bowls, and gadgets, jumped to her feet and dashed for the door.

Fergus, who hadn't yet left to return home, followed on her heels, then blocked her hand's path to the doorknob. "Don't just throw it open."

Where had her big-city caution gone? Molly nodded, then peeked through the side window.

Charlie Kinnaird.

The rage in his eyes made her take a step back.

Fergus glanced through the window as well. "Wow, young Charlie looks like he wants to fight."

He motioned to Molly and her partners, who had come running. "Stay back."

Molly didn't want to, but she allowed Fergus to open the door.

"Now Charlie, what's this all about?" he asked.

"I'm not here to talk to you, Mr. MacGregor." The young man muttered something unintelligible under his breath, then speared Fergus with questions. "Where are those women? The ones who told the police my mom or I killed my dad?"

"You're not talking to anybody until you cool off." Fergus started to shut the door.

But Molly darted in front of him. "Charlie, I'm Molly Ferris. Can I help you?"

The youth's bitter laugh grated on her ears. "Oh, you've helped us so much already." Charlie all but bared his teeth. "My mom was finally doing better. Then you and your friends had to open your big mouths about some stupid letter. Got her all upset again. But was that enough? No." He gulped a breath that sounded like a sob, then yelled, "You went and told the police we murdered my dad!"

"But we didn't—"

"Don't lie to me!"

Fergus drew Molly back and pulled his phone from his pocket.

"Charlie, lad. Calm down." Hamish had arrived, and he slid in front of Molly to face the boy.

Charlie's hysteria froze into a solid block of hate. "I heard you were on their side."

"I am on your side," Hamish answered gently, "as I have always been. I am also on the side of the truth."

"Right." Charlie practically spat the word.

"You and I are going to take a little walk." Hamish, wearing his teacher expression, grabbed his coat.

"I have nothing to say to you."

At Charlie's vicious tone, Molly repressed a shiver. Could the boy's thick jacket conceal a weapon?

Fergus also grabbed his coat, but Hamish shook his head, then nodded at the partners as if to say, *Stay with them.*

Fergus nodded. Hamish stepped onto the porch.

Charlie was muttering, "I hate him. I *hate* him." Molly couldn't help but wonder whom he meant.

Hamish pointed toward the lake.

Charlie—dark head hunkered into his coat, hands stuffed in

pockets—stood stock-still, then seemed to make a last-minute decision to join Hamish.

As the unlikely duo crossed the street, those remaining inside the bakehouse let out sighs of relief.

Fergus called the police. "Hello, Wilma?"

Molly winced. The receptionist would salivate at this story. "Do we have to—?"

"Absolutely," Fergus said with finality.

While he talked to Chief Thomson in clipped tones, Molly whispered to her partners, "We don't want to press charges, do we?"

They shook their heads in unison, and she touched Fergus's arm.

He paused and offered her his phone. "You want to tell the chief something?"

She took the phone and shared their viewpoint with the chief. "You're not going to arrest Charlie, are you? He's just a troubled kid who hasn't gotten over losing his dad."

"Well, if you don't plan to press charges, no. But for the record, we only questioned him and his mother when the letter surfaced. No accusations were made, yet it sounds like he was very threatening today."

Thomson cleared his throat, then said firmly, "I'm glad Hamish could handle things this time, but be sure to let me know if there's another problem with Charlie. Even a small one."

Molly promised, hung up, and handed the phone back to Fergus.

"Are you sure you want to let him go scot-free?" Fergus asked as he pocketed the phone. "What if Hamish and I hadn't been here?"

"But you were, and we appreciate it. We appreciate Hamish too." She darted to a window. "By the way, where is he?"

As if on cue, Hamish's tall, solitary figure reappeared down the street. A few moments later, he entered the bakehouse, looking drained. "I think he's calmed a bit," he reported. "But I'm not past my concern."

He sighed. "Easier to talk to them when they're little lads."

Though shaken by the incident, Molly, in her heart of hearts, hoped the troubled young man was innocent of anything more than misplacing his grief.

Before Charlie Kinnaird had darkened their door, Molly had mostly agreed to the Buchanan stakeout to keep an eye on Hamish and prevent him, Vernon, and Grizela from stirring up unwarranted trouble. However, as Fergus walked her to Grizela's house Friday night, she hoped against hope that they would learn something from watching John that would lift the burden of suspicion from young Charlie's shoulders.

Upon welcoming Molly, Grizela made no effort to disguise her joy in their task. "Come in," she said in a stage whisper. "We'll nail that no-good peddler of literary rubbish before the night's over."

The prospect of four hours with Grizela and her brazen glee almost made Molly turn and run, though the spring flower arrangement and bright red wicker chair on the porch lifted her sagging spirits a little.

When she complimented Grizela, the librarian aimed a fresh glare at John's house. "I paint it every spring. Not like some lazybones who never think about how their sloth affects the neighborhood. If only that sweet lad Kent were around more often." She sighed dramatically. "He's away fishing much of the year, but when he's home, he, Vernon, and my husband, Ronald, can talk for hours about whitefish." Her voice sharpened. "Can't hold a conversation for eight seconds with that other no-goodnik."

Molly wilted. Before Fergus turned to join Hamish and Vernon at their post along the shoreline near the bookshop, he offered a wink that said, *You can do this.*

She returned his smile, straightened her shoulders, and stepped into Grizela's pristine home. Molly sniffed the fragrance of freshly baked bread and immediately felt better.

"Just took it out of the oven." Grizela bustled into her 1940s galley kitchen. "Have a slice with butter and cherry jam. I picked the cherries myself last summer."

Perhaps this stakeout wouldn't prove such an ordeal after all.

"I sent a loaf with Ronald this afternoon to share with his fishing buddies," Grizela went on. "But the rest is ours for the eating."

She'd set up a small table as if for a dimly lit tea party next to a small, strategically located window lined in frost from the chilly evening. Peering next door, Molly could see John's run-down house—both entrances and most of the windows.

As she savored the delicious bread and drank tea from an elegant china cup, Molly mused that Grizela had likely conducted plenty of spying from this vantage point.

Between bites and sips, the librarian confirmed her suspicions. "See those dirty, side-by-side windows on the west side? The ones without curtains?"

At ten o'clock at night, I'm supposed to see dirt? But Molly nodded anyway.

"He always leaves a light on in that room—the dining room, I'm thinking—whether he's home or not." Grizela sniffed. "I shouldn't even mention the goings-on I've seen through those windows. Activities unfit for polite conversation."

"You've never been inside?"

Grizela recoiled. "Gracious me, no."

"Look." Molly pointed, dropping her voice to a whisper. "Is someone on the back porch?"

John's ponytailed silhouette had appeared, faintly haloed by another house's safety lights.

"There's that—that *criminal*," Grizela hissed. "Watch him. He's carrying something."

The man left the porch and headed toward the back alley.

Molly pulled out her phone . . . only to realize, on John's return to the house, that he carried a large trash can.

She'd been poised to report him for emptying the garbage? It seemed paranoia and suspicion were contagious.

Even Grizela couldn't find anything sinister in that, nor in his shaking dirt from a couple of rugs off the back porch.

When John locked his house and left, however, she brightened. "On his way to do some devilment, no doubt."

Or, like many single men on Friday evening, perhaps he was off to eat wings and watch hockey at an all-night sports bar. Nevertheless, Molly texted Fergus, noting John's exit.

We'll watch for him, he replied swiftly.

"You need more meat on your bones." Grizela served another warm slice of bread and jam onto Molly's plate.

A refusal would be considered an insult, so Molly gave in. Who could blame her?

Despite their remaining alert—or mostly alert—in anticipation of John's return, they didn't see him again.

Fergus and Hamish never saw him at all. "Tonight would have been more exciting if we could have watched the grass grow," Fergus told Molly and Grizela when he returned to walk Molly home at two o'clock. A stubborn Hamish had stayed on for a second shift with Harvey and Vernon.

The bookshop had remained quiet and dark. Vernon's "bad boat" crews appeared to have more sense than to sail on a frozen night like this.

Carol and Laura soon arrived for their shift. They talked Grizela into going to bed, then took their place at the spy window.

The next morning, they reported to Molly that they'd seen John return shortly before dawn, but he'd appeared to go straight to bed. Hearing that news from Carol, Harvey talked Vernon and Hamish into giving up their watch to go pick up Carol and Laura and head to the Bruces' to eat Joyce's big breakfast.

"We almost awakened you first shifters," Laura told Molly later, "but we figured you were dead asleep."

Molly chuckled ruefully. "After eating half a loaf of Grizela's bread, a big breakfast was the last thing I needed."

With Bread on Arrival's grand opening rapidly approaching, the Bakehouse Three couldn't afford to spend a morning recovering—even though their group planned another vigil that night.

"I feel a hundred years old today," Carol groaned, and the others answered with similar laments.

The prospect of baking together for the first time in the new kitchen, however, lifted their spirits. As a publicity tool, they were going to give away samples of hot cross buns and Easter cookies downtown. Soon, sheets of the treats filled the entire first floor with delectable scents.

They laughed and talked about old times as they stood shoulder to shoulder at the worktable, decorating bunny- and egg-shaped sugar cookies with pastel frosting and sprinkles. How long had it been since they'd shared the fun of baking together?

Once the icing on the hot cross buns and cookies was set, they loaded the baked goods into the hearse. Its paint and chrome had been polished to a sparkle, and the Bread on Arrival logo—a shortbread cookie bearing a Celtic knot design with their business name emblazoned across it—now adorned the driver's and passenger's side doors. Their phone number, website, and social media handles were listed on the back window.

Spiffed up or not, the hearse still hadn't won Laura over. She wrinkled her nose. "Have fun driving that thing."

"I will," Molly said cheerfully. After only a few lessons with Fergus and several practices, she and the vintage LaSalle had found their groove.

Cruising the busy downtown for the first time, the hearse caught the eyes of day-before-Easter shoppers. Occasionally, Molly parked to hand out flyers and the treats they'd baked.

With all the smiles, "yums," and phones aimed to take photos—hopefully shared on social media—the local campaign to advertise their business was off to a good start. The *Crown Press News* editor Molly had contacted sent a reporter to interview her and take photos at the table she set up in Dumfries Park. When Mayor Calhoun showed up at the park to try a bun, attracting even more attention, Molly couldn't help feeling a little guilty. So far, he'd passed every point of her scrutiny with flying colors. How could she benefit from the presence of a man she'd once considered a top murder suspect?

She accepted his best wishes with a smile and chatted for a minute or two, until his supply of pleasantries seemed to run out. Unlike Kinnaird, he didn't attract groupies, but overall, Tavish Calhoun appeared a solid citizen and caring mayor.

With the crowds thinning as dinner hour approached, Molly packed up her table, Easter decorations, and what little remained of the baked goods. A nap sounded wonderful, but maybe she should drive through outlying areas for an hour, letting the hearse do its visual magic.

Not before she treated herself to a stiff cup of coffee, however. After loading the LaSalle, Molly left it on the far end of the park and briskly walked to MacPhee's Family Drugstore, where she gratefully bought a large latte from the middle-aged woman at the counter.

The moment she left the store, she sensed someone watching her. Was paranoia taking over her life?

Molly, you really *need a nap.*

Still, she couldn't shake the impression.

The feeling grew stronger when she heard steps behind her.

Ridiculous. Another MacPhee's customer could be walking home along the same route.

Nevertheless, small fears swirled in her gut. She took a gulp of her latte, grimacing as it burned her throat.

The steps followed.

She fought the urge to glance behind her. *So he's parked close to the hearse.* Why should that shake her up?

When the steps continued, though, her heart sped up. Pulse pounding, she whipped around.

There was no one in sight.

She huffed a sigh that combined relief and exasperation with her own paranoia. Her imagination had certainly gotten the best of her. *It was probably my own footsteps*, she thought as she glanced down at her thick-soled shoes. Shaking her head, she walked the rest of the way to the hearse.

But when she saw it, she stopped dead.

A jagged, metallic gash ran along the car's entire side, slashing straight through the Bread on Arrival logo.

16

Molly had just finished reporting the incident to Chief Thomson when Fergus called. He knew immediately something was wrong, so, with a sigh, she related the story once more.

"You should stay home tonight," he said without hesitation. "The last thing you need on top of this is to participate in a stakeout and risk upsetting your harasser even more."

As if that were *his* choice. Molly's temper flared. "Look, this creep needs to understand that he can't intimidate me. That my partners and I are here to stay, whether he likes it or not."

After saying goodbye, she realized her words were braver than she was. A nap restored her somewhat, but as she prepared for their vigil, Charlie's dark rant the previous morning spread through her mind like an oil spill. If he was stalking her, what would the night bring?

And if Charlie wasn't stalking her?

They might witness John Buchanan's evil doings—or not.

And what if someone else was involved that she hadn't even considered? Her thoughts briefly alighted on Cameron MacPhee's anger at the mention of Mayor Kinnaird's death, and she connected it to the fact that she'd been at the drugstore when her car had been keyed.

Her thoughts tangled and knotted so she didn't know which she desired or dreaded.

Molly did know one thing: stalker or not, homemade bread or not, she couldn't stomach another four hours with Grizela. A phone call to Laura, who bartered future days off to substitute, assured Molly she wouldn't have to.

They made the switch without offending the librarian, with Laura insisting *she* wanted another privileged turn at Grizela's house.

Carol, who wanted to monitor Between the Pines with only Molly, encountered more opposition.

As the group huddled quietly near the lake before splitting up, Harvey crossed his arms. "Carol, I'm sticking with you and Molly. I don't want to hear another word about it."

Before Carol could argue, Molly intervened. "Why don't you take the lake watch closest to the bookshop? You'll only be a block away. And if you, Hamish, and Fergus are free to monitor the shoreline, we stand a better chance of success."

The men grumbled, but couldn't deny the logic.

"I don't like this, especially after the hearse incident." Fergus's frown deepened. "You'll text us if you notice anything odd, won't you? Anything at all."

Funny how she could feel warm on this damp, freezing night. "You know I will."

After they scattered, Carol murmured, "I love Harvey to pieces, but he's shifted into overprotective mode. We'll have more fun without him."

Molly snorted. "At midnight, I'll ask you how much fun this is—especially if the weatherman's right about a wintry mix."

"Shh. Don't even say it."

They hunkered in a small alley alcove across the street from Between the Pines. Though they couldn't see the back door, neither she nor Carol could find another spot that would hide them so well.

Molly whispered with a mischievous grin, "We could split up. I'll cover the back—"

"Are you trying to get me in trouble with my husband?" Carol whispered back. "Harvey will *sense* it if we split up. Then I'll have a 24-7 chaperone until the police catch the bad guy. Whoever it is."

"Which one? You mean the back-door burglar? The window-smashing vandal? Or the stalker with the keys?" Molly's levity faded as she remembered why they were here. "I hope we can at least help them catch the murderer—if there is one."

Carol nodded.

They laid the small vinyl cushions they'd brought on the frozen ground and sat down. For an hour, they heard nothing but the occasional rumble of a car or bark of a dog.

Ever since they'd settled in different cities, Molly had longed to spend quality time with her former roommate. However, she'd never envisioned their having to remain nearly silent for four straight hours. That exquisite torture was almost worse than trying to stay awake. Throughout their vigil, Molly gulped the potent coffee she'd brewed for the occasion. Carol drank hers as well, but lack of sleep the previous night and the day's work had taken their toll on both women. Molly was drifting off in spite of herself when a dim light gleamed for a few moments in the bookstore's window, then disappeared.

"Carol," she hissed. "Did you see that?"

"Sure did." Carol was already texting Harvey.

Molly bolted her gaze to the bookshop, but the windows remained dark.

Harvey, however, materialized in record time. Grimly, he joined in their vigil, and they resumed their surveillance.

After nearly another hour of staring, Molly's eyes ached. Her body protested at remaining immobile for so long. Maybe John had simply dropped by to check on things with a flashlight, then went home.

A perfectly normal action for a small business owner who awoke in the middle of the night, wondering if he'd forgotten to lock up.

They texted Laura. *Did you see him come or go?*

Haven't seen him at all, came an almost immediate reply.

When their shift was over, Fergus joined them, having relinquished his post to Vernon and Hamish. He and Harvey sneaked to the bookshop, then returned to report that they'd found faint boot prints in old snow by the back door. Unfortunately, they could have been made days ago.

Fergus's phone buzzed, and he answered it quickly. "Hello, Hamish. What? Okay. Be there in a sec." He disconnected the call and turned to the others. "Vernon and Hamish spotted a boat across the lake that appeared to be making its way toward the Dumfries Park pier."

"We're coming too," Molly said, knowing Carol and Harvey would agree. "Let's split up so they won't detect us as easily."

"We'll go in pairs, at least," Fergus said, then assigned Harvey and Carol to hide behind a utility shed located in the park's central area, where they could monitor a boat landing there or at the far end. Fergus and Molly would back up Vernon and Hamish near The Auld Crabbit and the park's pier.

"Stay safe." Molly hugged her friend before they hurried off into the darkness. She tried to match Fergus stride for stride, but he easily outpaced her.

The old men needed Fergus's help. "Don't be polite and wait for me," she urged. "Go on, and I'll follow."

He forged ahead, but still slowed his pace somewhat.

Why hadn't God given her long legs? Molly jogged, thankful she'd kept up some semblance of an exercise regime since moving to Loch Mallaig. In the dim glow of the park's safety lights, she kept Fergus in sight, watching him duck behind the canoe rental at The Auld Crabbit.

Trying to control the volume of her breathing, she crept from tree to bush to tree, then finally settled beside him. Phone pressed to his ear, he nodded at her, then murmured a goodbye to Chief Thomson as he pointed toward the lake.

The faintest of lights wobbled in the now-drizzly darkness. Closer and closer it floated, clearly making for the nearby pier.

With Fergus right behind her, Molly slipped into the shadows cast by the nearest building, a concession stand. They were so close to the lake that she could hear gentle waves lapping on the shore.

Her ears caught another sound. Laughter? Fergus perked up as well, so she wasn't imagining it.

Every moment, the light brightened and grew closer. Then it suddenly died, as did the mirth.

Molly caught her breath. Had the boat's occupants decided to turn around?

Moments later, a scraping sound against the pier and silhouettes climbing out of the large boat answered her question.

A powerful spotlight ripped through the night, illuminating the pier like in a movie scene. Chief Thomson's voice boomed through a bullhorn. "Stop! Police!"

Angry protests poisoned the night air as officers ran toward the boat. Shadows emerged from The Auld Crabbit, one protesting as the other hobbled toward the scene, pointing what was unmistakably a gun.

"Vernon! No!" Molly screamed.

Fergus sprang from their hiding place, but his intervention wasn't needed. Chief Thomson intercepted the old man, talking to him in a soothing yet firm voice as he took away the gun.

Weak with relief, Molly walked toward the pier, now swarming with a few officers and what appeared to be a group of young men and women. So this was one of Vernon's bad boats? Not exactly criminal masterminds, from what she could see.

Then she sensed something else and searched for its source.

Staring straight at her, hate sharpening his gaze, was Charlie Kinnaird.

His expression could have shriveled grapes into raisins.

Though Molly forced herself to keep her own face placid, her throat tightened until she could hardly breathe. She watched as the police questioned several of the boaters and determined they'd taken a parent's boat without permission. But was Charlie involved in something far worse than a late-night joyride with his friends?

Amid the commotion, the MacCallans appeared, with Laura and Grizela right behind them.

"I knew we'd catch that wretched Buchanan," Grizela crowed. "I just knew it." Scanning the group, though, the librarian paused. She cocked her head. "Where is he? Did police already take that *lochdach* to jail?"

"What lochdach, Mrs. Duff?" Chief Thomson's respectful tone told Molly he'd probably been *wheeshted* at the library before.

"Why, that bookseller who's behind it all," Vernon announced. "A liar, and probably a thief and murderer to boot!" He laced the comments with Gaelic words Molly didn't know and didn't want to know.

"That's enough." The chief's face grew stern. He cast a probing stare at their group and narrowed his voice to a penetrating whisper. "I know that letter has cast suspicion on half the town, but I can't even imagine why you think John Buchanan is involved in Mayor Kinnaird's murder."

Vernon and Grizela quieted. The others fidgeted. Molly found herself digging a toe into the mostly frozen ground.

Hamish couldn't remain silent long. "We were doing our civic duty as citizens of this town," he declared, gesturing at Molly, Laura, and Carol. "You know these ladies have suffered a burglary and vandalism, and today some wicked criminal damaged the bakery's delivery vehicle." He fixed the chief with a righteous glare. "Are we, who claim them as friends, to do nothing?"

"We are not doing nothing." Chief Thomson ground the words between his teeth. "My officers and I have worked many extra hours to investigate these cases. We will continue to do so until we've caught those responsible."

"And we appreciate your work and protection," Molly said, while the others echoed her gratitude.

The chief's expression didn't soften. "Regarding Mayor Kinnaird, we have no evidence that he was murdered, let alone who did it." Frustration saturated Thomson's voice again as he glanced from one person to another. "Why on earth would John Buchanan be involved?"

Molly, Fergus, and the MacCallans exchanged sheepish glances. Even Hamish held his peace.

Grizela and Vernon, however, grabbed the opportunity to tell the chief exactly what they thought about the bookseller.

Cautioning them to keep their voices down, Thomson listened. However, his shoulders stiffened in exasperation with every word. He was clearly unconvinced, and Molly couldn't help but agree. What had they all been thinking, suspecting a nice man like John Buchanan of murder?

When the irate seniors paused for breath, Molly asked, "Chief, do you mind if we go home?"

Thomson nodded. "Go. I'll make sure these two get home. But please let *us* do the stakeouts from now on, okay?"

Heads lowered, they trudged back to their cars.

"Hot chocolate at my house." Laura almost made it sound like an order. "If we don't unwind, we'll never sleep."

Nobody seemed to mind adjourning to her cozy, cheerful cottage.

As an apology to her exhausted body, Molly topped her steaming mug with a double dose of whipped cream. Plopping into one of Laura's overstuffed chairs, she repeated the question that had looped through her mind a few dozen times since the lake episode. "What do you think of Charlie's being out in a boat this time of night? Was that more than just a bunch of kids partying?"

"I can think of more fun things to do on a Saturday night than freezing to death on the lake," Carol answered.

"As if we didn't do our fair share of midnight boating when we were younger," Laura teased.

"Back when staying out all night was to be expected," Fergus said wryly. "I doubt Owen was amused by our stunt."

It didn't take great insight to know he felt foolish for the whole situation, which made Molly feel worse. She and her partners were newcomers, and, in the chief's eyes, bound to make a few blunders after a burglary and vandalism. Hamish, though a life resident with a proper Loch Mallaig pedigree, was an eccentric whom no one could predict.

Fergus, however, was a pillar in the community, a businessman not expected to participate in unsolicited stakeouts and make random accusations of murder.

Molly patted his shoulder. "I'm sorry you were pulled into this."

He blinked. "You didn't drag me into this. I want the three of you to feel welcome and safe in our town. With some nut or nuts pulling stunts—well, I can't stand by and watch."

His words warmed her more than the hot chocolate. "Thanks."

"Thank you, Fergus," Carol echoed. She raised her mug, and Harvey, Laura, and Molly followed suit. "And you too, Hamish."

The handyman acknowledged their gratitude with a nod. "While I won't wave a gun at night boaters like Vernon, this sort of thing cannot be allowed in Loch Mallaig. I won't rest until we track down this hooligan. Whoever it is."

"So," Molly said as she gazed around at her friends. "What next?"

"I think we need a break," Carol announced. "Tomorrow's Easter, after all. I want to spend it at church and with my family."

"Backing off—for a day, at least—might be best," Fergus agreed. "I'm going to the sunrise service, and then we'll be extra busy with the Easter brunch at the King's Heid. I should be at Castleglen to help Neil."

Fergus's selflessness the past two nights struck Molly anew. "How will you stay on your feet?"

He shrugged off her concern. "After all these years, I'm used to the Easter crowd. Wouldn't know how to act without a hundred people lined up at our doors."

Hamish, however, still frowned. "I am all for celebrating the Resurrection, but those who do evil will not stop even in honor of the holiday. I cannot help but feel we should press on."

His phone rang, and the others had to remind him to answer it. They could only hear half the conversation, but given Hamish's spluttered, "But, lass, I—" it couldn't have been going his way.

After he hung up, stuffing the offending phone into his pocket, Hamish's expression said it all: Joyce had vetoed any investigating on Easter. He drew himself up in a stern effort to have the last word. "We'll discuss this again on Monday."

While we're all running around madly, preparing for the grand opening on Saturday. Molly stifled a tired sigh.

As she drove back to the bakehouse, Molly hoped Grizela and Vernon would also relax their vigilance over Easter. She shuddered, thinking the night could have ended much worse. Vernon might have blown a hole in the kids' boat. Thank goodness the chief had dealt with him so well.

Had she and her friends accomplished anything related to their troubling mysteries? Not really.

Weariness settled over Molly, so heavy that even Angus's delighted greeting didn't make the everlasting trip up the stairs any easier. When she opened the office door to make sure she'd turned off the new computer, the Scottie dashed to the window and barked as if the view of a sleeping downtown and shoreline were a brand-new sight.

"Shh, Angus. Enough already." Grabbing his collar, Molly glanced out the window—and realized she could see farther than she'd thought. Her gaze landed on the pier.

A light, faint but unmistakable, shone at the edge, then vanished.

Clasping her dog, Molly dove into bed and covered her head with every pillow and blanket she could grab.

17

"Christ the Lord is risen today. Alleluia!"

Molly sang along with the church choir and congregation, letting the joyful message and music wash away the toss-and-turn anxiety of the night before. So what if strange lights had dotted her sleep? God was with her, and she wouldn't fear the future.

Laura, harmonizing beside her, reminded Molly that despite Chloe's having to stay in Milwaukee—a junior vet was on call for holidays more often than her senior partners—she certainly was not alone. Carol and Harvey had invited both her and Laura to share in their family's Easter brunch and egg hunt. Afterward, their entire group would adjourn to the Mighty Scot Marina for another pontoon ride with the Bruce clan.

The MacCallans' seven-year-old twin grandchildren, Maisie and Gavin, welcomed them with open arms when they spotted Laura's Easter coffee cake, resplendent with pastel flowers and fragile, molded butterflies.

"Are you magic? Like the Easter Bunny?" Maisie's chocolate-colored eyes had widened until they rivaled the eggs in her basket.

Nothing like two lively kids zipping around Carol's soggy but sunny backyard to help the previous night's bizarre episode fade from Molly's mind.

At the marina, however, Hamish's dour whisper brought it all back with a vengeance.

Scanning the peaceful blue water, dotted with numerous boats full of happy families, he shook his head. "Vernon is right, you know. Evil is abroad, and it never stops until someone stands up to it."

"Hush." Joyce pulled him away. "The little ones will want to fish a bit during our ride. They need help with their poles."

Despite her efforts to distract him, Hamish issued a litany of gloomy statements throughout the afternoon—each a little louder than the last.

"We could all join forces to push him overboard," Laura finally suggested under her breath.

"We may not need to." Molly gestured toward Joyce and Tanya, who wore similar vengeful expressions. "Hamish ought to worry a little more about threats closer to home."

Still, the beautiful afternoon and the children's fun—Alannah and Gavin caught a fish apiece—loosened the tension. Though Molly was tired when they docked the pontoon, it was a good tired, one she hoped would generate an early bedtime and peaceful night. When Vernon didn't show up to add his own dire warnings to Hamish's, she breathed a sigh of relief.

However, Logan appeared puzzled as he helped his family disembark. "Didn't Vernon say he would meet us here to help tie up?" he asked Tanya. "Can't remember the last time ol' Vernon didn't show up with his latest bad news."

"Your dad's supplied enough for one day," his wife muttered. Always the kind hostess, though, she invited everyone to the snack bar for a light supper of sandwiches.

Joyce insisted that Hamish eat with his family instead of driving over to The Auld Crabbit to check on Vernon as he wanted.

"I know what will happen if those two get together tonight," she told Molly and the others. "Hamish will be gone half the night cooking up conspiracy theories, and it's not happening on Easter—not when he promised to spend the evening with the girls and read them a story before bedtime. Vernon's probably talking fish with Kent Donner or Ronald Duff. Nothing to fret over."

Molly turned to Tanya. "I appreciate your hospitality," she said in answer to the dinner invitation, "and you've all made my first Easter in Loch Mallaig so special. But after all the Easter goodies I consumed today, I couldn't eat one more thing."

Although Laura offered to spend the night, Molly actually craved a little alone time. Besides, in spite of her less-than-honest exchanges with Chloe, she missed her daughter and couldn't wait to call her.

Cuddled with Angus on her love seat, Molly fed Chloe a detailed recap of her wonderful Easter and a lively description of their plans for Bread on Arrival's grand opening—all the while still omitting any details about ongoing investigations.

Chloe had attended a service with friends, and then they'd all shared an elegant Easter brunch at a historic downtown hotel. "Mom, I can't help thinking of how much you're missing, living in the middle of nowhere."

"It's a wonderful place, dear," Molly said, not for the first time. "You can't imagine how beautiful it is here. Let me know when you can come visit, and I'll show you."

Despite her invitation, she really, really hoped Chloe would stay occupied in Milwaukee for a good while—at least until the letter issue was resolved. Hanging up, Molly realized the evasion had simultaneously drained her of energy and robbed her of the pleasant sleepiness the day had brought on.

That'll teach you to keep things from your kid, she told herself grimly. Though no hungrier than before, Molly jumped up from the love seat. "Come on, Angus, let's grab a snack, then go for a ride."

More than happy to comply, the Scottie dashed for the kitchenette. Since it was Easter, Molly threw him two treats and nibbled on a heavily sprinkled egg-shaped cookie the MacCallans' grandchildren had baked for her. Having made quick work of his snack, Angus followed her downstairs and outside to her Honda.

No one's keyed it, thank goodness. With a slight shiver, Molly peered into the back seat before opening the door. Angus bounded inside and settled himself on the passenger side.

"Let's take the scenic route tonight," she told him as she turned toward Lake Superior. "If we hurry, we might catch the sunset."

Molly headed toward a boat launch and picnic area ten miles away that she'd noticed on her way into town once. She'd park in the nearby lot and watch the golden sun swirl his colorful robes about him before retiring like some exotic potentate.

With the evening chill returning and the wind kicking up over the lake, few cars remained in the lot. Molly smiled, then sighed at the sight of a fiftyish couple paused arm-in-arm and heads together, with the sunset and lake as a romantic backdrop. Though Kevin had passed away more than a decade ago, she still missed him—

Wait.

Molly slowed, then parked at the nearby picnic area instead. Quickly, she snapped on Angus's leash and hurried among the trees toward the lot.

The couple still lingered—a tall man and small woman.

Cameron MacPhee and Fiona Kinnaird.

Molly's memory played back images in close-up detail—images that apparently meant more than she'd realized.

In the newspaper photo with Cameron's enormous smile, the photographer had caught him aiming it directly at Fiona. And hadn't he stuck close to her—in a camouflaged sort of way—at church?

The hint Molly should have caught, however, was Fiona's early-morning visit to Cameron's business. That was definitely more than an errand.

Charlie's raging face floated among the other images. Could he have seen his mother leave the drugstore and worked out that she was dating Cameron? Had that friction detonated the primeval fury Molly had seen as Charlie entered the store, perhaps aiming to confront Cameron? *So maybe it wasn't about me at all.*

Nor was his outburst at the bakehouse front door. "I hate him," Charlie had mumbled, over and over.

She had supposed that the troubled kid had meant those words for his dead father. But had he actually meant them about his mother's new love? A man who represented everything his father had opposed? *Slow down, Molly.* How many times had she told herself that lately? She pushed away the thoughts and let Angus lead her to the nearest bush. Yes, Charlie probably knew about his mother's relationship with Cameron and loathed it. She shivered. Perhaps the pharmacist had better watch his back too.

Even as Molly's logical side reasoned, the word pharmacist echoed through her mind, refusing to ebb away.

Pharmacist.

Someone who could aid a desperate spouse in manipulating medicines and covering up lethal doses so a coroner wouldn't detect them. Or who could potentially do it all by himself.

Someone who, perhaps, saw the chance not only to rid the community of a political scourge, but reclaim the woman he'd loved for years. To quietly eliminate the popular guy who'd stolen her from him back in high school.

While Molly tried to shake off these unpleasant thoughts, Fiona and Cameron separated with clear reluctance, glancing back at each other as they unlocked separate cars. Cameron waited several minutes after Fiona left, probably so no one would see them drive back into town at the same time.

Molly doubted the two, regardless of feelings for each other, had carried on an affair before Kinnaird's death. Neither Betty, Jane, Wilma, nor Doreen had even hinted of such goings-on, and the gossip network certainly wouldn't have missed something so juicy. No, their outright dating must be fairly new, or Wilma would have broadcast it throughout the UP by now.

Molly's head continued to spin as she and Angus returned home. She couldn't begin to think how she would share this new development at tomorrow's regrouping discussion—nor how the news would be received.

She didn't want to think, period. "Don't let me go into the office," Molly told Angus as she rinsed and filled his water bowl. "I don't want to look out that window."

No staring at the pier. No flashlights, imaginary or otherwise, tonight.

Hamish's words floated through her mind. *Vernon is right, you know. Evil is abroad, and it never stops until someone stands up to it.*

"Shut up," Molly said aloud.

Angus cocked his head, but didn't let her tone distract him from lapping away at the fresh water.

Why hadn't Vernon showed up to help tie the boat? He seemed like the type to be true to his word. Though if he had been caught up in conversation with other fishermen, perhaps he'd lost track of the time.

Still unsure, Molly told herself that it wouldn't hurt to peek out the window toward The Auld Crabbit. If lights were on, surely everything was fine.

Except they weren't.

Not only was the little bait shop a dark blob in the night, but the light that usually illuminated the pier had been turned off. Molly touched the glass with an uncertain finger. Was Vernon keeping vigil for John alone tonight, gun in hand?

Molly shook herself, as if that would disperse the worries that jammed her mind.

"You're lucky," she told Angus. "One good shake, and all's right in your world."

Molly visited the window twice more. The second time, she saw a flashlight shining against The Auld Crabbit's siding. Was that Vernon?

Or could the old man be in trouble?

She had to find out. As Molly donned her parka and grabbed a flashlight, she considered texting her partners or calling Fergus or Hamish.

But they'd insist on joining her.

Which was exactly why she wouldn't contact them. Why should their Easter end on a paranoid note? Especially Fergus—he'd given so much, and he'd probably worked without a break at his resort today. It would be unfair to wreck his sleep just because she couldn't relax. Hamish would be on board, but his wife wouldn't, and she had no intention of antagonizing Joyce. She was a wonderful ally, and Molly wanted to maintain that status. Laura, Carol, and Harvey were probably going to bed, if not already asleep. They'd all gotten far too little rest over the last few days, and she didn't have the heart to wake them.

Besides, surely nothing was actually wrong. She just needed to see that for herself so her brain would let her rest tonight.

She shivered as she left the bakehouse. The sky, so full of sunlight and springtime promise during the day, now glittered with countless ice-chip stars over the lake. With the dropping of temperatures, the ground crunched under her feet as she approached the shoreline.

At night, the bait shop looked even more dilapidated than during the day. With no light inside or out to warm its sagging frame, the tiny shack appeared as desolate as if it had been abandoned decades ago.

She passed the beam of her tiny but powerful flashlight through the dark windows. No evidence of a break-in. No helpless old man lying on the floor, either in the front or back room. Molly tried the door, but it was locked. She rapped gently. "Vernon?"

No cranky old man stormed forward to answer.

Vernon's fishing boat bobbed by the pier—thank heaven he wasn't out on the lake at night, searching for evildoers.

Vernon must have planned to be gone this Easter. He simply hadn't told anyone.

But he promised Logan he'd meet them at the marina.

Molly killed her light and hushed her noisy conscience with a mental reminder to show up early tomorrow to check on him. In doing so, she'd probably make Vernon her enemy for life. Right now, that prospect didn't bother her at all, not if she could reassure herself that he was okay.

She'd almost talked herself into going home when her gaze rested on the bookshop, and a glimmer caught her eye. Then another.

Two more lights flashed far out on the lake.

Molly caught her breath.

Her feet propelled her toward the bookshop before she could decide what to do.

She hunkered behind a large dumpster at the far edge of Dumfries Park. Did she see movement in the bookshop's parking area? Was this the evidence against John Buchanan that Vernon, Hamish, and Grizela had craved?

Or was Molly about to help disrupt another spring break party?

She winced. Before calling Chief Thomson, she'd check around a bit, try to nail down a solid reason for her concerns. Molly slipped from evergreen to bare-branched bush to building, finally flattening herself alongside a shed behind the bookshop.

No streetlight illuminated the small parking lot, so she saw little but shadows. Those shadows, however, resembled the shapes of men. Were they carrying large duffel bags toward the park?

Molly slithered along the wall for a closer look—

An explosion of pain detonated in her head, stars darted across her vision, and then she knew no more.

18

Waves of throbbing pain. Waves of nausea.

Drifting on a foggy sea of agony, Molly detected toxic voices far away, yet much too close. Unfamiliar men spoke words that made no sense.

Her stomach lurched, but Molly's head injury sucked her back into an ebb and flow of consciousness. Finally, she remained alert enough to realize that she lay on an unmerciful surface that pressed into her spine—the deck of a boat, and it smelled nauseatingly of fish. When she tried to turn, her hands and feet, bound tightly with duct tape, refused to budge.

"What were ye doin', lad, runnin' guns right past our very noses?" Vernon's voice, coming from maybe a few yards away, sharpened her muddled brain.

Guns? What did guns have to do—

"Not on my beautiful Loch Mallaig, ye don't, criminals!" the older man hollered. A dull thud ended the old man's defiance.

No. No.

Facing the wall of the boat, Molly couldn't see the assault, but she felt it radiate through every bone in her body.

"Why didn't you just gag him?" The voice sounded mildly annoyed.

A nasty, gravelly chuckle answered. "He'll be more cooperative this way. Don't you think, Donner?"

"I suppose."

Donner? With sickening certainty, Molly realized the identity of her captor—John Buchanan's tenant, Kent Donner. That explained the suspicious lights at Between the Pines. The fisherman likely had a key to the shop since he worked there part-time, and he could have easily borrowed John's leather coat for his late-night antics.

Donner lowered his voice, but Molly heard his next words far too well. "I'll have to figure out what to do with her, anyway."

"You'd better." No trace of mirth remained in his fellow conspirator's voice. "They're your problem. Just so you know, I don't intend to do more time."

"You won't, if you do what I say." Donner's tone hardened.

"Listen, I know you think you're king of this operation," the other growled. "But you couldn't do it without us. Who collects the guns for you from Chicago and Detroit so you can make the deliveries to your Canadian friends?"

"You'd never have made the connection if I hadn't laid the groundwork and taken care of key people on both sides. I've done it all for years without anyone raising so much as an eyebrow. Small-town guy, everybody's fishing buddy, likes to keep the lawn neat—that's me."

Molly gritted her teeth to keep from spouting what she thought.

"That *was* you for a while," the gravelly voice cut in. "But not anymore. The end started when that mayor caught on to us."

Molly froze. A mayor who'd found out about their guns?

Douglas Kinnaird!

"You took care of him," the other man continued, "but you didn't play it smart with that battle-ax librarian or this old geezer. Now you got *bakers* on your tail—and mine. What did you do?"

"I'll handle it. And you'd better handle it too, Mason." Donner's tone sharpened to a deadly point. "Remember, I've never gotten so much as a parking ticket. You, on the other hand, are still running from armed robbery charges. Start getting the wrong ideas, and one phone call could take you out of the picture. There are plenty of others who'd be happy to work this cushy gig I've set up."

Silence.

"Let's not fight about this." Donner's voice regained some blandness. "You've always done good work for me. I know you'll do whatever's needed for us to succeed."

"As long as you make it worth my while." Mason wasn't backing down.

"Have I ever shorted you?" Donner asked. "If you take care of these two, there will be something big in it for you. Really big."

This time, Mason's silence reminded Molly of a wolf about to pounce. "All right," he said at last, "but you better come through."

Their murmurs of lethal negotiations faded as they moved to the other side of the boat. Negotiations that would result in death for Vernon and Molly as they had for Kinnaird?

Molly closed her eyes tightly, as if that would keep her mind from supplying vivid pictures of her non-future.

A short while later, Molly overheard terse exchanges between Donner and Mason as they stomped on and off the boat, apparently moving more duffel bags. Finally, she heard Donner say, "I'll call the others, let them know we're on our way to meet them."

The boat's engine purred to life—*he must have paid extra for a quiet motor*—and Molly realized they must be sailing to meet another boat. She thought about the men's previous discussion and figured the other boat was on Lake Superior. Were they really running black-market guns to Canada?

She recalled the article Harvey was writing. He'd mentioned that Canada's strict gun laws were carefully enforced at border crossings and in more populated areas. Once runners in the less-patrolled UP sailed across Lake Superior, however, the Canadian wilderness probably presented a much easier entrance for illegal guns from the U.S.—and the possibility of enormous profits.

Despite the dark night, Molly caught sight of Vernon's bait shop as the boat glided smoothly along the Loch Mallaig shoreline toward the McLain River, which would lead them to Lake Superior.

At the thought of poor Vernon, who remained silent where he'd been struck, rage rose in Molly. Anger without a plan, however, accomplished little. After breathing slow and deep, she tried to channel her wrath into a strategy. She cursed the fact that her friends had no idea where she was, then realized that her captors didn't know that.

She flopped over to get Donner's attention, the impact sending lightning bolts of pain through her head. Despite seeing stars, she got her first look at the man, and realized that he resembled John Buchanan fairly closely. She hadn't noticed it in the photos at the snack bar. Had he intentionally chosen to rent from a man he looked like? It had certainly worked in his favor, since Vernon had mistaken one for the other.

"So you're awake." Donner sounded a little bored. "Bad luck."

Molly shook with fury, but managed to temper her tone. "You're the one whose luck has run out. My friends will follow us."

"Really?" Donner gestured with his head. "Unlike Saturday night, you were alone when Mason over there found you snooping around the bookshop. You've been on my boat for an hour. How soon do you expect your friends to come running?"

"Any moment," she flung back, though her heart sank.

"Oh, I'm sure they're all in bed, tired from that nice boat ride you took earlier." His knowledge of her day's activity sent slivers of ice through her veins. "Don't think the police will help either," he continued. "They've got to keep an eye on all those college kids back on spring break, like the ones you busted having a party last night. Yes, the cops are spread very, very thin this week."

When Donner's phone buzzed and he stepped away to answer it, Molly tried to catch sight of any surroundings that would give her a clue as to their location. The silhouette of a tree overhung the water on one side. Another big, skeletal shadow appeared on the opposite side. The boat must have reached the river.

"What?" Donner barked. "Where?"

Molly perked up her ears.

"Get another boat out there *now.*" Donner stomped to the other end of the boat, so she couldn't hear the rest of the exchange as he hissed and muttered. Even in the darkness, though, his tall figure stiffened.

Someone knows.

The realization lit the gloom like a candle.

The boat, which had been creeping along, sped up. Molly's rush of relief was cut short when powerful hands yanked her from the boat's floor.

"Let out one peep, and I'll knock you right back out," Mason snarled. "Just like I did that old geezer. Or maybe I'll chuck you overboard."

Molly knew Donner wouldn't let Mason do that, not with someone pursuing them. Nevertheless, her lungs tightened into knots as Mason carried her into the foul, fishy hold. The man tossed her onto a hard bunk, stuck a cloth gag into her mouth, and covered her, head and all, with a heavy, musty blanket. Not a sliver of light touched the smelly darkness. She heard a loud thump. Had he brought Vernon down too?

"Pleasant dreams." Mason's gravelly snarl left her shaking with terror.

Still, someone knew. Didn't they?

Molly wriggled with all her might, and the blanket slid down. She still couldn't see a thing, though. Gradually, her twisting and turning lessened to an occasional despairing yank on her duct-tape bonds.

Trying not to gasp, she lay still a moment. No doubt the drawers in this fishing boat's hold concealed any number of sharp knives, but they might as well be a thousand miles away. Molly gathered herself, then flopped until she lay facing the hold's wall. Little by little, she inched along, exploring it with rapidly numbing fingers.

No nicks or sharp edges materialized on which to rub the duct tape.

Head throbbing, she almost gave up and went to sleep. A small lump in her pants pocket, however, irritated her hip.

Keys.

The scum upstairs had confiscated her phone, of course. But they hadn't bothered to take her keys.

By now, her efforts had stretched her arms and wrists until they felt nearly wrenched from their sockets. Still, she managed to secure the keys, determine the key with the roughest edge, and scrape it haphazardly against one of her bonds.

Molly dug and rubbed, barely smothering a cry when the key accidentally jabbed her flesh. The slow inefficiency of it all tempted her to quit—

Until she replayed that horrible voice in her mind. *Pleasant dreams.*

Until she thought about Chloe. Her parents. Her friends and their dream.

You may think you've won, and maybe you will.
But you haven't beaten me yet.

The gentle lapping of river water as the boat sped along soon gave way to teeth-rattling lurches. The boat's bow slammed into Lake Superior waves that jounced Molly so hard, she feared she'd hit the floor. Angry winds moaned, then screeched outside, almost drowning shouts above.

On the positive side, she detected frantic, heavy footsteps and strained shouts above. Donner and his accomplices were panicking.

On the not-so-positive side, Mason thundered into the hold and yanked her from the bunk.

Molly's keys flew from her deadened hands.

He guffawed. "You planning on driving away?"

His beefy fingers, however, detected the small gap the key had rubbed in her wrist bonds.

"Trying something, are ya?" he snarled.

He shook her so hard she couldn't have answered if she wanted to, then furiously wrapped fresh duct tape around her wrists.

"Hey, we don't have all night!" Donner yelled down into the hold. "Bring the old man up too."

Tossed over Mason's shoulder, Molly was carried to another boat, then dumped into the arms of another hulking henchman. This man took Molly to another dark, fishy hold, and covered her with a similarly revolting blanket. The familiarity was not comforting.

She choked down a sob as her new captor returned, hauling someone else—presumably Vernon—into the hold.

As the bigger boat accelerated, she clung desperately to her last vestige of hope. Someone knew. Someone was following.

Weren't they?

Wind howled outside. Rain assaulted the deck above. Growing waves slammed against the side of the boat.

Even if a rescue was in progress, would her liberators brave this storm?

The increased heaving of the boat, despite its size, and the loss of her keys dragged her morale down as if she were already tied to cement blocks.

How long she lay in throbbing, nauseous misery, she didn't know.

She only knew the waves were lifting the boat so high Molly wondered if they were actually flying. The corresponding plunge slung her off the bunk, crashing her against the floor.

A silent, lead-heavy body dropped on top of her.

Vernon.

Dead?

Please, no.

With every muscle, every cell, she struggled to free herself, but she simply couldn't.

Crack! Crack! Crack!

A barrage of gunshots ripped through the night.

A rescue? Joy swelled in Molly, but fear's icy dagger shredded it. Would the gunshots tear through the boat's hull? Would freezing water gush in, stealing whatever life might be left in Vernon? In her?

Fight, her brain commanded. *You can loosen those bonds!*

Her bruised, sleep-deprived body, now limp as seaweed, refused. Did she hear water sloshing into the boat?

Chloe, I love you.

Father, into Thy hands, I commit my spirit . . .

Loud, garbled words boomed above the wind's hysterics, battering her fading prayer.

The boat shuddered to a stop, but Molly, sinking into oblivion, didn't wonder why.

She barely caught the rumble of an unfamiliar male voice before a single beam of light above her brightened, then vanished as if blown out forever.

19

"Molly? Are you all right?"

Fergus?

She recoiled. He couldn't be working with Donner, could he? Even as her dazed mind conjured the impossibility, she rejected it. Flashlights beamed in her eyes, dazzling them shut.

"Hurry," another voice urged. "Let's get them out of here."

The men shifted the heavy load from her body. Strong arms picked her up and held her securely as they emerged from the hold. The blast of cold air that met her felt like heaven, and spotlights illuminated her surroundings—including her rescuer. Fergus.

Fergus carried her to the boat's side, where an inflated life raft fought to hold its own in the wild water. He handed her to a huge man with rough hands.

Too much like Mason. The gag choked her cry.

"It's all right, Molly," Fergus reassured her, then vaulted into the lifeboat beside her. He grabbed a blanket—one that smelled like fabric softener, not fish—and draped it around her, trying to shield her from freezing spray as the raft battled through the water toward a larger ship. His warm hand gently pulled the gag from her mouth.

She gulped sweet, icy air as their craft sped up. "Vernon?" Molly gasped.

"He's alive. He's in the other lifeboat." Fergus pulled out a pocketknife and began working on her bonds. "Once we make it to the police boat, we're taking you both back to the medical center in Loch Mallaig."

"Thanks be to God." Hamish's familiar voice caught Molly's ear.

"You kept saying evil was abroad." She started to shake her head, but stopped when the throbbing intensified. "You were right."

He nodded. "Usually am."

The matter-of-fact statement was so wonderfully, blessedly like Hamish that—for the first time in what seemed forever—she chuckled.

Predatory waves still clawed at the little lifeboat. As to the hows, whens, and wheres of the rescue, Molly had no idea. For now, though, Fergus's comforting arm helped to ward off the chill and let her believe she was safe.

The words "thank you" seemed like a teacup that couldn't begin to contain the ocean-size gratitude she owed her friends.

But she said them anyway.

Lying on a bed in the chilly emergency department of Loch Mallaig's Kinnaird Medical Center, Molly didn't want to look Chief Thomson in the eye as he approached her. She fully expected an epic rebuke for her unsolicited, solitary stakeout.

"You're looking better," he said in greeting, his tone kind.

"I'm feeling better," Molly replied with a small smile. "They're watching me for a while, but I've just got a mean headache and some bruises. It could have been so much worse." She paused. "Thanks for your part in rescuing us."

The chief apparently read her mind, issuing a tiny smirk as he allayed her fears of a scolding. "I'm not going to reprimand you tonight. I'm too thankful you're all right." He cleared his throat. "Any chance you're up for a short interview?"

Frankly, Molly didn't want to acknowledge that the past five hours had actually happened, but she nodded anyway.

"What's the most important thing you saw or heard?" he asked. "Besides being rescued, that is."

Molly took a shaky breath. "I think it was when Donner and Mason were talking. They were arguing, and Mason said something about Donner blowing their cover, that 'it all started when that mayor caught on to us' and that Donner 'took care of him.'" Molly tried to stop shivering. "Do you think Mayor Kinnaird found out about Donner's gunrunning operation? And then Donner killed him?"

"I never would have believed it before," the chief admitted, "but now that I know he's a gunrunner and a kidnapper, that seems more than likely." He patted her cold hand. "I think that's enough for tonight."

He turned to go, but Molly grasped his arm. "Coming back on the police boat, I thought I saw Mason and maybe some of the others in custody. But I didn't see Donner." She tried to steady her voice. "Was he in the hold? Is—is he in jail?"

"I wish." Chief Thomson's poker face fell. "That guy avoided risking his own neck whenever possible. He didn't join you on the Lake Superior boat. He just sent you and Vernon ahead with his buddies. He managed to land his boat in a little bay, then took off on foot."

Molly's throat tightened. Donner was still out there?

Eyes flashing, the chief leaned forward. "But don't worry, Molly. Every police officer in Michigan is looking for Kent Donner. The Canadians are watching too. We'll get him. Soon."

"I know." She fell back against the pillow and into a deep, dreamless sleep.

When Molly awakened a couple of hours later in her own recovery room, the nurse told her she had company. Molly cringed, both craving and dreading the arrival of her partners.

"Just what did you think you were *doing?*" Carol's tight-mouthed outrage was harsher than even her teacher voice.

"If you weren't already half dead, I'd kill you." Laura looked ready to do it.

Their fierce hugs, however, conveyed their true feelings—relief and love.

"I'm only a quarter dead," Molly joked. "The doctor is already working on my discharge papers."

Laura raised an eyebrow. "Think you can stay out of trouble for a few hours before getting kidnapped again?"

"I didn't exactly intend to get kidnapped," Molly said. "I couldn't sleep last night, and I saw a flashlight at The Auld Crabbit. I was just checking on things. I wanted to make sure Vernon was all right since he hadn't shown up to help with the pontoon boat."

"Maybe the next time you 'just check on things,' you might call one of us?" Carol pursed her lips.

"I will," Molly promised. "Hopefully, the most dangerous thing I'll do from now on is teach Laura how to drive the hearse."

Laura laughed and hugged her again. Laura's lack of witty retort and the relief still so plain on her face told Molly how deeply her abduction had affected her friends.

She looked from one to another. "I am sorry. Hopefully, there won't be a next time. But if there is, I won't go it alone."

"Good," Fergus said from the doorway, and Molly wondered how long he'd been there. "We'll hold you to that."

Molly's heart caught in her throat for a moment as she locked gazes with her rescuer. Not trusting herself to venture into sentimental territory by thanking him, she said instead, "Chief Thomson told me the basic, official version of what happened. Anyone want to fill me in on your side of things?"

Hamish scooted around Fergus to approach Molly's bed. Always eager to inform, he grabbed the opportunity to report on the night's events. "As you know, even as we took the children fishing on Logan's pontoon yesterday afternoon, an uneasiness pursued me that I could not deny. I had hoped to warn you all away from danger." He stared pointedly at Molly. "I should have known better."

Good grief, she'd never hear the last of this. "I know, I know. But you couldn't shake it either?"

Hamish grimaced. "No. I was especially concerned about you being alone last night. When I couldn't sleep, I went to the bakehouse and inspected the yard. No one answered the front door, so I used the keys you entrusted to me and entered. When only Angus answered my banging on your apartment door, I let myself in. It was past midnight, but you were nowhere to be seen, and that little dog was beside himself." He sounded as if he was scolding a teenager for missing curfew.

"How did you find out about Vernon?" Molly asked, ignoring the chastising tone.

"I saw from your windows that his lights were off," Hamish said. "Even his pier light. That's when I called Fergus."

Fergus nodded. "I took my motorboat over to The Auld Crabbit. I couldn't rouse Vernon either. Right after Hamish joined me there, we saw flashlights at the bookshop. We hoofed it over there, but by the time we reached it, nobody was there. We went back to the shoreline, but Donner's fishing boat was already out into the loch."

"You must have missed me by minutes." Molly couldn't believe it.

Fergus rubbed a hand over his eyes. "If we'd been just a little earlier, we could have stopped anything from happening to you." His tone was heavy with regret.

"You did. I'm still alive, aren't I?" Molly smiled encouragingly. "And for that, I'm eternally grateful. How did you catch up with us?"

"We went back to the bait shop, jumped into my boat, and took off after Donner's boat." He shook his head. "I wish we'd called Chief Thomson earlier, but we didn't know for sure who we were following."

Molly glanced at Hamish. Like her, he'd hesitated to risk calling in another party bust.

"We didn't want to jump the gun," Hamish agreed, "but the longer we followed that boat—our lights off too, of course—the more we wondered why it was out this time of night with no lights. When we heard its motor head down the river toward Lake Superior, we called the chief."

"Apparently he'd had officers randomly scoping out the shoreline after the party incident," Fergus said, "but they didn't report anything suspicious. Fortunately, he took us at our word and called border patrol."

"I wonder if it was an officer's flashlight I saw down at the bait shop," Molly mused, somewhat to herself, thinking that she might have had a different night altogether if her run-in had been with a police officer instead of Kent Donner. Was he in custody yet? She fought the fear prickling at her, knowing she was in the safest place she could be.

While she wrestled with the sense of unease Donner's fugitive status instilled in her, Fergus continued the tale of her rescue. "With the storm kicking up, my boat couldn't have handled Superior. Even the police boat had a rough time in those waves and had to slow down. They did pick us up at the mouth of the river, though, so we got to help get you away from those . . . those . . ." Fergus's words died, but the frozen flames in his eyes told them all exactly what he thought of her captors.

Hamish picked up the tale. "Between the gunshots and the storm, their boat was taking on water, big time. You and Vernon were tied up and helpless." Emotion settled in the wrinkles of his face. "You could have drowned."

Molly patted Hamish's arm. "I'm fine now, thanks to you both. It's Vernon I'm worried about." She swallowed. "What did they do to him?"

"The cowards hit him far harder than one would need to subdue a man of nearly eighty." The softness Hamish had fleetingly shown flared into anger. "Smashed his face to a pulp."

Molly flinched and shifted the conversation. "Can we see him?"

Fergus shook his head. "Vernon's under observation. They may have to transfer him to the trauma center. We can't get in to see him because we aren't family."

Carol's eyes sparked. "Did you tell them he has no family in the area? We're as close to family as he has."

Grizela appeared then, though she didn't bustle into the crowded room with her usual take-charge demeanor. Molly had to assure her several times that the doctor had said she'd be fine, and even then, Grizela seemed quite uncomfortable.

"Is something bothering you, Grizela?" Molly asked gently.

"I suppose I have to eat some crow, don't I? Accusing John Buchanan of evil when it was really Kent Donner." Grizela shook her head, toying with her purse straps nervously. "And when Mayor Kinnaird died, I just knew something was wrong. I should have told Chief Thomson immediately what I saw. Then maybe that devil and his demons wouldn't have hurt you." Her eyes reddened. "Or Vernon."

Molly hated the pain in the librarian's face. "Do you want to tell us about it?"

Grizela rubbed a tired hand across her forehead, then nodded. "Late one evening, I saw Mayor Kinnaird standing at John's front door. Not unusual, as the mayor often visited the people of the town. Still, I did not understand why he would come to see *him*." Her usual contempt for John returned, but it quickly vanished in a flash of embarrassment. "Thinking back, I never actually saw the mayor talking to John. It was clearly Kent he came to see. I heard a terrible argument between them, and I should have told the chief about it."

"While that might have been helpful, I doubt the police would have considered it at all conclusive," Fergus reassured her, and the others echoed agreement.

Grizela's mouth twisted. "Still, when Mayor Kinnaird died not long afterward, I figured John was behind it. But I also knew the police wouldn't believe me, so I wrote the letter you found. I hoped someone at the wake or service would read it and act." She shook her head, her gray curls bobbing. "Being double-minded is never good. At first, I put the letter in the mayor's casket. Then I wondered how anyone would find it there. I took it out. Then I put it back. Then, when I heard Hamish returning from answering the front door, I stuffed the letter into the cabinet and tried to forget about it." She sighed. "When you girls bought the funeral parlor, I panicked."

Hamish glared at her. "Is that when you broke into these hens' bakehouse? And used that spray paint to make it look like a teenager did it?"

"Yes. That was inexcusable." Grizela's chin sank to her chest. "How I wish I'd used that paint to put another coat on my red wicker chair instead. Still, I had hoped to retrieve my letter before it caused problems."

"It did stir things up," Molly admitted, covering Grizela's hand with her own, "but if you hadn't written the letter, would anyone have questioned the mayor's death? Would the police have discovered Donner's gunrunning?"

Grizela shrugged.

Molly raised her eyes to the librarian's sad face. "Your methods weren't without flaw, and you may have had the wrong guy, but ultimately, you brought the truth to light."

"Thank you." The tears in Grizela's eyes finally escaped as she turned to face Carol and Laura too. "Though my actions have caused you so much trouble, I hope you all will forgive me."

Carol patted Grizela's arm. "Of course we do."

"We wanted to repaint that siding anyway," Laura added.

"God bless you," Grizela whispered. Then, patting away her tears with an old-fashioned lace handkerchief, she straightened. "I must go to the police station immediately to tell the chief what I did. I will pay for the damage, and I'll try to make it right. No, I *will* make it right."

She marched out, a woman on a mission.

For a moment, Molly and company simply stared.

"Make things right?" Fergus's eyes twinkled. "Bet none of you will pay an overdue fine for the rest of your lives."

"Don't count on it." Unlike Grizela, Joyce did bustle in, giving Molly a big hug. "Grizela would only give a freebie like that to God, and even He better not overstep."

Once more, Molly marveled at how the woman's presence instantly made any day—even this one—better.

Before the conversation could continue, Molly's phone, which had been returned to her by the police, rang. She grabbed it from the bedside table.

Chief Thomson's strong voice boomed across the line. "I wanted you to be one of the first to know that Donner's in jail."

Molly closed her eyes. *Thank you, Lord.*

Her friends, sensing the call's importance, quieted as she asked, "Where did they find him?"

"At the Houghton County airport, trying to leave in a small bush plane," Thomson said. "Apparently he'd talked a buddy—or maybe threatened him—into taking him to Canada. The police stopped them just as the plane was rolling onto the runway."

"Thank you for calling me." Molly felt relief flooding her. "There are still a lot of bad guys out there, but it's nice to know there's one less loose in the world. In Loch Mallaig."

"Exactly how I feel. Get some rest now, Molly. We'll talk later."

After the call, Molly brought the group up to date about Donner's capture, then suddenly felt bone weary. Perhaps she could fit in one more nap before her discharge papers came through.

While the others discussed the case, her eyes drooped. She didn't resist the velvety fog drifting over her. Surrounded by some of her oldest friends and two of her newest, Molly drifted peacefully into a slumber so pure, she felt weightless.

20

Whoever thought a dream come true would begin at three a.m.?

It was the morning of Bread on Arrival's grand opening. Fortunately for Molly, the fragrances mingling in the kitchen compensated for the early start. Piling yet another stack of used pans in a sink, she paused to inhale chocolate, citrus, and vanilla scents, heightened by one that surpassed them all: the rich, comforting smell of freshly baked bread.

Carol, loading buttercream-frosted layer cakes on a cart, followed suit. "Hey Laura," she said to their hardworking friend. "Stop for just a second."

"What?" Laura glanced up, but her hands still moved in a blur, scooping muffin batter into pans.

"Before time gets away from us, let's all take one huge sniff together to celebrate our bakehouse," Carol suggested.

Molly followed Carol to Laura's prep table. "Strikes me as a great time for a group hug too."

They joined arms and stuck their noses in the air.

Carol counted, "One, two, three."

Along with the others, Molly took a giant breath in, then hummed appreciatively on the exhale. Lost in the yummy fragrance, they inhaled again.

"I don't want us to ever forget this incredible moment," Carol said.

"We won't." Molly pulled out her phone and aimed it for a selfie. "Hug close and sniff again."

"I'd better not see this on the Internet," Laura warned.

Checking the photo afterward, Molly couldn't repress a giggle. "You're right, our noses aren't meant for publicity purposes. But we look like we're having fun."

"We'll have Harvey take the official one." Carol returned to her cart of cakes. Molly picked up a tray of petit fours to put in a display case, while Laura returned to her muffin batter.

Hamish, who had shown up at five, poked his head inside the kitchen door. "I need someone to help me level this banner."

"Coming," Molly said. She slid her tray into the bakery case, then following him onto the front porch, where a vinyl banner was hung loosely from nails on either side of the entrance.

"Tell me when it's even," Hamish instructed as he climbed the ladder to adjust one end.

Molly wandered out onto the sidewalk to assess the hunter-green banner with plaid around its edges. Large white letters in a Celtic font read, *Welcome to Bread on Arrival's Grand Opening.* In the expanding morning light, the front beds of blooming daffodils, lined with fragrant blue and pink hyacinths, created a picturesque welcome.

"It's perfect, Hamish." She grinned. "The balloons I have on order will be just the right finishing touch."

"Balloons?" Hamish nearly spat the word, and Molly was glad he didn't fall off the ladder in his rage.

"What's wrong with balloons? They're festive."

"They're nonsense." He eyeballed her.

She eyeballed him right back.

Muttering under his breath, her handyman climbed down the ladder.

She summoned her best smile. "It'll draw attention to the gingerbread trim you worked so hard to repair and paint. The whole place looks wonderful, Hamish."

He grumbled again as he stood beside her on the sidewalk and took in the view, but he couldn't seem to oust the grin from his face. "Aye, it does look nice."

Molly could have reveled in the sight all day, but a bakery's grand opening, unlike most stores, didn't wait until ten in the morning. Before she went back to work, she asked Hamish about Vernon, who had been moved to a better equipped hospital in Marquette.

"Saw him yesterday. Still weak, but doing better. Has enough energy to gripe about being tricked by that Kent Donner. Stubborn old fool may come home soon." Hamish harrumphed. "They'll throw him out just to get rid of him."

Hamish hadn't insulted Vernon since before his injury. Such reassurance brought yet another smile to Molly's face. She hoped Hamish could tell her good news about Charlie too, no longer a suspect in his father's murder, and Fiona, now free to get on with her life. "Have you talked to Charlie?"

"The boy's settling some," Hamish said, "and he agreed to get counseling when I told him he's still fighting with his father." The handyman shook his head. "Maybe it will help Charlie come to terms with Cameron's courting his mother too. Right now, he can't see her side at all."

"At least he doesn't have to fear they killed his dad." Molly felt a jolt of embarrassment that she'd ever suspected Cameron or Fiona, but she whisked it away with a simple wish of happiness for the couple. Her heart lifted as she turned to survey the cloudless sky. "I do believe it'll be warm enough today to bring out the topiaries and other plants."

Within minutes, she and Hamish had arranged them all on the porch and front steps, adding spring-colored cushions to wicker chairs and the swing. She clapped her hands. "The porch looks just as I pictured it the very first day I saw it."

"You've all worked hard."

Molly blinked. *Was that a compliment?*

Before she could recover, a cheery "good morning" grabbed her attention.

Grizela, panting a little, held a large box. "Hamish, will you carry this inside the bakery? I brought my special dishes for the girls to use in their grand opening."

Surprisingly, Hamish complied without complaining. Perhaps he'd decided that fighting with women today wasn't worth it.

Molly, however, couldn't remember arranging for this loan. Nevertheless, she politely said, "Thank you, Grizela."

"No problem at all. I didn't want you to run out. Banner's looking nice." Grizela went inside without invitation.

Molly stifled a sigh, knowing the librarian had set her course for the bakehouse kitchen. Earlier this week, in efforts to "make things right," Grizela had proved quite helpful, washing piles of dishes as the Bakehouse Three hurried to begin fulfilling their contract to supply Castleglen with bread and desserts for the King's Heid Pub and its smaller sister bistro, Tee for Two. No doubt, she'd prove invaluable today—if she stuck to washing dishes.

In addition to attempts to reorganize their supplies, Grizela had given Laura advice on making bread. Laura, the former head chef at New York's elite 29 North restaurant! Molly cringed at the memory. Her friend had not taken kindly to an amateur tinkering with her recipes, leading to a frosty tension in the bakehouse.

Now, though, as Molly reentered the main room, she breathed a sigh of relief to see the librarian working well with Carol. Together they'd stocked the section of a case devoted entirely to Scottish treats.

Hamish emerged from the kitchen, where he'd left the box of dishes, and the display drew him as if he were six years old. He identified each delicacy by name: the buttery, currant-dotted Selkirk bannock, the caraway-flavored Abernethy biscuits, the Empire biscuits, which consisted of two iced shortbread cookies sandwiched with jam. A parfait-like treat, however, sent him kneeling almost reverently before a refrigerated case.

"Cranachan," he murmured, wide-eyed at the small faux crystal dishes, filled with layers of raspberries, cream, and oats. "Those look almost as good as my mother's. Where did you find big, lovely raspberries like that this time of year?"

Laura, carrying more goodies from the kitchen, smiled at him. "It took a little doing, but I have my sources."

Hamish pulled out his billfold. "Let me be your first customer."

When he refused to let them give him the dessert, Molly took a quick photo of him making the first official purchase at Bread on Arrival.

"You're forever preserved for posterity," she told him.

His feelings about balloons aside, Hamish had proved himself invaluable, as usual. As Molly decorated their tables with small vases of fresh tulips he'd arranged, she noted he'd situated the blossoms exactly as she had asked. He'd also dusted until she couldn't find even a speck.

In addition to the tulips, pots of daffodils and ferns brought natural vibrancy to the rustic Northwoods furniture and the shining hardwood floor. More color splotches dotted the floor, courtesy of the morning sun shining through the stained glass of the front door's brand-new window. A skilled artist they'd found in Copper Harbor had not only created an intricate design depicting loaves of bread and Celtic knots, but he had also tracked down authentic early 1900s glass with which to build the replacement—and done it all in record time.

"That guy really did a bang-up job." Harvey, who had just arrived with backup supplies from local grocery store The Hamper, seemed especially glad the plywood had been replaced.

Molly examined the highly polished antique display cases, now bursting with decadent baked goods of every kind. Surely they rivaled those found in much bigger cities.

Along with Molly's balloon delivery, more plants and flowers arrived, sent by the local chamber of commerce, Lochside Realty's Beverly Scott, and Castleglen Resort, whose card was signed by Fergus and Neil.

"How sweet of them." Molly buried her nose in multicolored lilies. Carol elbowed her. "Are these for all of us? Or just for you?"

"I'll bet Neil doesn't even know his name's on them," Laura teased.

However, the bouquet that topped them all—an arrangement of tulips, hydrangeas, and roses—left Molly wordless and fighting tears.

At the sight, Molly's partners bestowed hugs and tissues. "What's wrong?" Carol asked. "Who's that from?"

Molly showed them the card.

Congratulations. We're glad you followed your dream.

Love, Mom, Dad, and Chloe

Laura clapped her hands. "I told you they'd get over it."

"What's this at the bottom?" Carol squinted at the card. "'P.S. We forgive you.'"

Molly laughed, then choked on a sob.

Chloe, of course, had read news accounts on the Internet of Molly's abduction, Donner's gunrunning, and the probable murder of Mayor Kinnaird—whereupon she had informed Molly's less cyber-savvy parents of her mother's activities. Angry, tearful phone calls had followed, with Molly apologizing a hundred times and promising that, from now on, she'd tell the truth, the whole truth, and nothing but the truth.

After an explosion or two, her parents seemed ready to forgive. Chloe, however, had cut off all communication—but her signature on the card, even if it was put there by the florist, was a sign that she'd eventually come around.

Powered by the promise of reconciliation with her daughter and an absolute certainty that she was right where she was supposed to be, Molly experienced a rush of joy she hadn't felt since before Kevin had passed away.

Joy that even Donner, with his ugly plans and uglier actions, couldn't destroy.

When Reverend Findlay and Bonnie arrived a little before opening to bless their business, Molly was more than ready to give thanks. Holding hands amid the circle of partners and friends, she saw they too, shared her wonder and gratitude.

"Thank you, Lord, for preserving these our sisters through difficult times," the pastor prayed. "Please continue to strengthen them. Make them a blessing to our community, and their bakehouse a place where the joyful and the weary alike can celebrate Your goodness."

"Amen," they chorused.

Mayor Tavish Calhoun arrived a short time later to cut the wide plaid ribbon stretched across their front door. He marveled at the main room's makeover, complimenting their hard work and forecasting great success for their business.

"After all you've been through, I hardly feel worthy to do this," he said as Molly handed him a pair of scissors. "Please join me, ladies."

Molly didn't dare look at Carol or Laura. How could they have suspected this mild, pleasant man of murder?

"We'll be glad to," Carol said.

Molly went to the kitchen and brought back three more pairs of scissors. Followed by Hamish, Grizela, and Harvey, they walked to the front door and opened it. A cheer went up from the growing number of customers standing in line.

Mayor Calhoun made a few remarks—brief seemed to be his byword—then turned to Molly, Laura, and Carol. "Ready to open Bread on Arrival for business?"

The Bakehouse Three exchanged triumphant, loving glances. Neither the years, nor the miles, nor the challenges had quenched their dream of working together.

Flexing her scissors, Molly answered for all of them. "Oh, we're ready."

21

A rush of triumph surged through Molly as she deftly snipped the ribbon. Would anything stand in their way now?

Along with the mayor, she, Carol, and Laura waved to their first customers. "Welcome to Bread on Arrival," Molly called out.

Wilma Guthrie waved as she zipped inside. Cell phone plastered to her ear, she was already reporting her take on the bakehouse's grand opening. Carol managed to direct part of her attention to the baked goods.

Jane Thomson, a close second in spreading town gossip, darted inside, then around the room, hands pressed together in ecstasy. "You've made this so cheerful, so lovely. Such pretty dishes too, holding those muffins and breads. They look exactly like Grizela Duff's."

"She was kind enough to loan them to us," Molly said.

"Oh. She didn't tell me that." Jane surveyed the case with hungry eyes, then pointed. "Those pies look delicious. I must have that one. Blueberry, right?"

Molly hadn't expected one of their first customers to buy *her* specialty. Maybe she could contribute more than just event-planning expertise and dishpan hands after all.

She was glad, though, to see that Jane also snapped up one of Laura's chocolate tortes and a strawberry mascarpone cake. Upon hearing that her tenant was enjoying the crofters' cottage, Jane beamed and bought a dozen Scottish snowballs for her husband. "They're filled with jam and dipped in coconut, you said? That's perfect. He doesn't like chocolate. Though what's not to love about it, I don't know."

Molly smiled. "I hope your family enjoys the variety."

"Oh." Jane laughed and peered into the large bag Molly had packed for her, as if sharing her sizable purchase hadn't occurred to her. "It looks like your tempting goodies got the best of me."

Enjoying the mental image of Jane digging into the pie, cake, and torte solo, Molly turned to welcome their next customers. Gratified to see several unfamiliar faces, she found out they'd witnessed her downtown promotion the day before Easter. Hopefully, these new friends would spread the word about Bread on Arrival.

Her heart warmed as more townspeople, as well as many customers from Houghton, Lake Linden, and even Copper Harbor, flooded the room.

"Everything's selling," Carol exulted. "You did a great job of publicizing us, Molly. Plus, plenty of out-of-towners are coming because they read about the Donner case." She grinned. "Several have called us the Bakehouse Detectives."

"Yeah, being kidnapped was all part of my PR strategy," Molly deadpanned.

She had to admit, though, that the bizarre events of the past weeks had increased their flow of patrons far beyond any expectations.

Today, not only Loch Mallaig's *Crown Press News* and Houghton's *The Daily Mining Gazette* had sent reporters, but also Marquette's *The Mining Journal.* Fortunately, Hamish, Grizela, and Joyce filled in at the counter when the partners were answering questions or posing for photos.

One reporter asked Molly, "You know they exhumed Mayor Kinnaird's body, right?"

"Yes, Chief Thomson keeps us informed," she answered evenly.

Facing heavy prison sentences, Donner's partners had told the police all they knew. Donner had followed Kinnaird to the restroom after the town meeting, knocked him out at a sink, then injected the mayor with potassium chloride, a drug whose effects not only mimicked the effects of a heart attack but also its laboratory chemistry. Donner, like most of Loch Mallaig's population, knew Kinnaird was diabetic and that the drug injection site would likely escape the coroner's attention, since Kinnaird had also taken insulin injections. The knot on Kinnaird's forehead had been attributed to his fall after the supposed heart attack.

Now, of course, Donner was claiming that his partners had threatened him and forced him to hold up his part of the operation. Molly doubted that, and she imagined a jury would too—especially since the police had called in the FBI, having found a connection between Donner and a terrorist group.

"Aren't you the one who led the authorities to Kent Donner?" another reporter asked Molly.

"Er, sort of?" Molly replied. The fact that she alone of the Three had been kidnapped evoked a hundred questions from the reporters and crowd that gathered. Molly, who really didn't want to remember the terrifying moments on the kidnappers' boats, answered inquiries patiently for a while, then deferred to Hamish. "I was tied up in the boats' holds, mostly out of it. Our friends Hamish Bruce and Fergus MacGregor were the ones who initiated the rescue and participated in freeing Mr. Pennycook and me."

Hamish, happy to give a personal account, held his audience spellbound—while Molly gladly returned to bagging cookies and oatcakes.

Thankfully, the arrival of Laura's parents, her brother, Brody, and his family from Marquette, restored the atmosphere from news briefing to celebration. Jenny and Craig brought Carol's ecstatic grandchildren too. Maisie and Gavin spent the better part of ten minutes competing to find the cookie with the most icing.

As her partners hugged, laughed, and joked with their families, Molly couldn't help feeling a twinge of envy. They'd moved closer to their loved ones. Her move had almost driven hers away.

The flowers they'd sent, though, said otherwise. As she mingled, bagged, boxed, and replenished, Molly touched the faceted glass vase or sniffed a bloom whenever she passed the bouquet that rested near the cash register.

When Logan and Tanya's clan arrived, Molly's temporary blues vanished. Nothing like the hugs and chatter of four little girls to dispel that solitary feeling.

Then Fergus came and bought Molly's one remaining blueberry pie. "Whoa, that's the last one? From now on, whenever you bake them, reserve one for me, okay?"

"Will do." She aimed a teasing smile at him. "After all, if you hadn't helped us find this building, we might have waited forever to start our bakery. Even worse, I might not have learned to drive a stick shift."

"That would have been so sad." Fergus's eyes twinkled, then sobered. "How did the repair shop do on the LaSalle?"

"It looks like Donner's goon never touched it." She chuckled wryly. "Chief Thomson said that even the guy who confessed to keying it regretted that he had to damage such a classy-looking car."

"That it is. I'll have to check it out before I go." Fergus's lightheartedness faded. "I still can't stand the idea that those thugs hurt you."

Enough of Donner, already. "Hey, we won. They lost. We're following our dream. They're in prison." Molly beamed at Fergus. "Seriously, without you and your help, Bread on Arrival still might be only a pipe dream."

"I like helping make dreams come true."

Molly had to drop her gaze and hope the heat creeping up her neck wasn't visible.

Fortunately, Neil, who also had shown up, interrupted to offer his congratulations.

"Thanks so much for coming by, both of you." Molly clasped Neil's hand. "We know your busy season is kicking in."

"Busy season for you too," Neil observed. "Yet you sent our first order on time. One less thing to worry about this weekend."

With a smile similar to his dad's, Neil snapped up a chocolate croissant and headed back to the resort.

"Guess I'd better go too." Fergus sighed. "Lots of work to do around the golf course." He grinned. "Does your slice still give you trouble?"

"Every time." Molly made a face. "Some of us weren't born and raised on a golf course."

"Well, come over, and I'll cure it for you. Guaranteed."

"Sure, in my spare time. And yours."

"Ah, we have to relax sometime. Don't forget about our Welcome to Summer bash. And sometime soon, we'll all escape from business and have a picnic on Lake Superior, where no one can find us."

"You're on." She waved goodbye, then scurried to help bring out more Scottish treats from the kitchen. Thank goodness they'd baked and frozen extras, because their fresh stores were rapidly diminishing. Laura had stationed herself in the kitchen, icing and decorating newly defrosted cakes and cookies.

Molly had just brought out fresh strawberry pies when the sight of two new customers edging toward the pastry cases halted her in her tracks.

Charlie and Fiona Kinnaird.

A hundred words sprang to her mind, but her mouth wouldn't cooperate.

The late mayor's wife and son paused, faces blank.

Finally, Molly muddled through a greeting. "Welcome to Bread on Arrival."

Charlie wandered a little to the left, staring at the nearest wall. Though still sad, his eyes no longer looked haunted. Or angry.

Fiona took a step forward, still glancing from side to side. "My, my. You've changed everything." Was she recalling her husband's wake here?

"I suppose we have," Molly said.

"It really is pleasant. Sometimes change can be a good thing."

"It can." Molly swept a hand toward the pastry case. "May I help you find something?"

Fiona bent to inspect the display. "I can't wait to sample your breads. I like a good, crusty bread even better than cake or cookies."

Glad for an easy topic of discussion, Molly launched into descriptions of the Scottish breads Laura had made and indicating where each was located.

"They look and sound wonderful." A small smile blossomed on Fiona's thin face. "I might need a while to make my choices."

"Take as long as you like."

Fiona nodded and leaned closer. She whispered, "Thank you."

For what? Warmth crept up Molly's face. *For resurrecting your pain, casting suspicion on you and your family, sneaking around trees to watch your romantic rendezvous?*

But Fiona murmured, "For finding out the truth."

With that, she hastened toward another showcase.

Whew. Molly thought she'd earned a reprieve, but as Fiona moved away, Charlie sidled up and took his mother's place.

She hadn't known what to say to Fiona. Talking to Charlie seemed unthinkable.

But before she had to come up with something to say, he spoke first. "Nice place here. Lots better than an old funeral parlor."

"Thanks." She tried to summon her brightest smile.

His lightly stubbled chin sank toward his chest. "I came because

I wanted to say I'm sorry. You didn't do anything wrong. I just got mad. I didn't want people to blame my mom for Dad's death. I didn't want them to blame me either." His voice faded until she had to bend forward to hear. "I shouldn't have thrown that rock through your window. That was stupid on so many levels."

Thomson had traced the vandalism to Charlie, but Molly and her partners had decided he'd been through enough.

Now the young man mumbled, "Thanks for not pressing charges."

"You're welcome" didn't quite fit. Instead, Molly murmured, "I'm sorry you lost your dad. And I'm sorry all this stirred up pain for you and your mom."

He nodded. "At least, we know what happened now. And who's to blame." For a moment, a fierce light shone in his face. "Donner won't get away with what he did to Dad. To Mom and me. And what he did to this town." The young man's voice broke. "We may have had our differences when I was a teenager, but Dad really was a good mayor."

"Everyone seems to know that."

For a few moments, Charlie stared at the scones as if they were the answer to all his problems. Then he muttered, "I haven't had my job very long, so I don't have much money. But maybe I could help Mr. Bruce around here to pay for the window?"

The prospect of both Charlie and Grizela "making things right" raised questions in Molly's mind, but she said bravely, "I think my partners would appreciate that. Talk to Hamish and see if it can be worked out."

"Thanks." For the first time, a ghost of a smile, not unlike the late mayor's, crossed Charlie's face. "I'd better find my mom. She'll buy all the healthy stuff, you know. I want to get at least one thing I like." He turned hastily and headed for the rainbow rows of cupcakes and giant chocolate chip cookies.

"I assume that went well?" Carol had apparently watched them from another counter.

"Yes," Molly said. "I'm so relieved."

"But wiped out. No wonder, with your family stuff and the reporters, and now, the Kinnairds too." Carol gave her a gentle push. "The crowd's thinned out a little. Take a break in the kitchen. Eat something that isn't sugar. Then the rest of us will take a turn."

After putting up her feet for fifteen whole minutes, Molly did feel better. When she reentered the bakery area, she saw John Buchanan gazing into a display case filled with an assortment of globally inspired desserts not from Scotland, including French pastries, Mexican wedding cookies, Black Forest cupcakes, and more.

Because John had shared a house with Kent Donner, the police had investigated him, but they'd cleared him of any wrongdoing. In fact, Donner's illegal activities had been carried out mostly when John had either been overseas or attending all-night poker tournaments in Marquette, as he had the night of the first stakeout. Donner had worn John's leather coat whenever possible as a safeguard against being identified while moving the guns in and out of the bookshop basement, which he'd used as a temporary hiding spot.

"See something you like?" Molly asked as she reached the display case.

John nodded, his ponytail bobbing. "I'll take a piece of baklava. My mother used to make it like that. She brought her grandmother's recipe from the old country."

Molly grabbed a bag and a piece of tissue. "Your mother was Greek?"

"My parents immigrated to Nova Scotia before I was born," he said. "My dad worked in international shipping and he landed a great job opportunity there."

"But your last name is Scottish," Molly mused as she retrieved his baklava from the case.

John laughed. "The name on my mortgage and bank statements is Giannis Bykhovetz. Doesn't exactly roll off the tongue in a wee Scottish town like this, does it?"

"Not exactly. But you know, there's nothing wrong with being yourself." Molly felt a flutter of understanding. *At least now we know why we didn't find an obituary for Diana Buchanan.* She grimaced. Had Grizela sensed this small fib and let it develop into an all-out vendetta against the man? Hit by a sudden rush of guilt for having suspected the bookseller capable of murder, she added another piece of baklava to the bag and handed it over. "On the house, Mr. Bykhovetz."

As John walked away smiling, Molly's ear caught the skirl of bagpipes outside. Alastair had promised he would come and play, though he wasn't sure about recruiting others. Had he found more pipers who could join him?

Given the rapidly rising volume, including thundering drums, the head of The Piping Yoopers must have succeeded. Stirring music was just the thing to get Molly's blood pumping again.

Laura had joined several customers near a window. "Hey, great job, Molly. I didn't know you'd lined up the dancers too."

"I didn't know I had either." Molly strode through the front door, followed by her partners. Out on the lawn, several pipers, including Alastair Thomson, Greer Anderson, and Mayor Calhoun, and two drummers played their instruments, all wearing full plaids. As The Piping Yoopers puffed and pounded, six dancers—led by a grinning Dallis—jigged and leaped.

The Bakehouse Three waved from the porch and clapped with the music. When a number of spectators joined in the dance, Molly, moving closer, knew she had to capture this moment for her family. Holding up her phone, she took a video of the fun scene.

Apparently, though, Dallis had decided she and her partners shouldn't remain bystanders.

As he danced toward her, kilt pleats swinging, Molly clasped her hands behind her back. "No, Dallis. Remember my three left feet?"

In answer, he whirled her into a circle of dancers, and Molly found herself trying to imitate the others, doing something that resembled a combination of square dancing and the Highland fling.

She tried to escape several times, but Dallis never failed to grab her hand and pull her back in. Molly stumbled, she whirled—the wrong way—and she promenaded with Dallis and two other men who probably hoped they'd never see her again. Breathless with laughter, Molly finally collapsed at the end of a song.

"What—what was that?" she gasped as Dallis helped her to her feet.

"Just a wee reel. Come, that's only the first part." He tugged on her elbow.

"No, that's the *last* part for me. The. End." Molly thanked the musicians and the dancers before escaping to the porch. There, Joyce and Harvey were trying to conceal their amusement.

Hamish, however, was bent over, roaring with laughter. Finally, he panted out, "Lass, you're a woman of many talents. But dancing is not one of them."

And tact isn't one of yours. But what did she care? She'd had fun.

When Laura and Carol, far better dancers, returned after the reel's end, Molly said, "Boy are you two in trouble now. Dallis won't give you one moment's peace until you join his dance troupe. I, on the other hand, am undoubtedly safe."

"You certainly were memorable," Carol tried to reassure her.

Laura didn't bother with diplomacy. "I saw lots of phones taking videos. You'll probably go viral."

Molly hoped Chloe wouldn't see *that*.

She forgot about Scottish reels, though, when she spotted a wheelchair, pushed by a middle-aged woman in scrubs, as it slowly rolled up the sidewalk. Despite pleasant weather, the wizened, pale-faced man sitting in it clasped a heavy blanket around his shoulders. His hazel eyes, though, looked as indomitable as ever. He fussed at his nurse, who gazed heavenward more than once.

"Vernon." Hamish beat everyone to the wheelchair. "And what are you doing here, ye old fool?"

"Thought I'd come see a bigger fool," the old man retorted.

"We're so glad to see you out of the hospital, Vernon," Molly interjected. "I can't believe you made it to our grand opening."

"Ye didn't let those hooligans get the best of ye," the bait shop owner said, "so I couldn't let them get to me."

"Welcome home, Vernon," Laura said kindly. "May I bring you something to eat?"

"He can't have any sugar," his nurse said. "Or fat. Or caffeine—"

"Who do you think you are, the Almighty?" Vernon groused. "I'll have whatever pleases me."

Together, they talked him into warmed slices of oat bread.

"Tasty," Vernon admitted. "A thousand times better than anything this infernal hen forces on me."

"This 'infernal hen' wants you to get well," his nurse flung back, "so I can forget I ever saw your face."

They were still arguing as she pushed him back to her SUV.

Molly exchanged worried glances with her partners. "Goodness, do you think that's going to work out?"

Hamish chortled. "It's working out splendidly. She makes him mad enough to fight. As long as ol' Vernon wants to fight, he'll live." He waggled a finger at Molly. "I wouldn't be surprised if he beats the doctors' predictions all to pieces."

It made sense, in a weird sort of way. And Hamish certainly knew Vernon better than she did.

Molly and her partners served the remaining customers inside and, observing the time, began to prepare for closing. Since their ceremonial opening had been later than their standard opening time, they'd extended business hours this first day. Many customers and curious passersby lingered outside, even after they finally locked the door. Since they'd be closed the next day—although they'd likely be in the kitchen replenishing their stock after church—the Three and their helpers didn't have to scrub everything spotless immediately. Molly, Laura, and Carol insisted they alone would come in the next day.

"If you show up, we'll lock you out," Carol threatened.

Hamish, grinning, held up his set of keys.

Oh. Right. He could open every door in the place if he wanted.

For once, though, Hamish looked weary. "Aye, it's been a long day. Joyce and I may take you up on that."

After hugs and many expressions of thanks, the helpers left just as Harvey arrived with Angus, who'd spent the day at the MacCallans', and a slow cooker of steaming Scotch barley soup. Molly retrieved a few remaining oatcakes from the case, and they all tucked into a hearty dinner, well deserved after a busy day.

After supper, Molly and her friends rested on the front porch's cushioned chairs and reflected on their journey thus far. The dream they'd followed and for which they'd worked so hard had come true.

Molly cuddled Angus on her lap, loving his furry warmth. "Pinch me," she said to her partners. "Did we really just celebrate our grand opening?"

Laura obliged playfully. "Why didn't you think it would happen? Just because we were burglarized—"

"And vandalized," Carol added.

"And I was kidnapped by a gunrunner who had murdered the town's mayor? I don't know why that might interfere." Molly perked up her ears as bagpipe strains of "Amazing Grace" floated from the town square.

"How appropriate," Harvey said. "It's God's grace you and Vernon are still alive. And that this whole bakehouse thing didn't fall apart," he added with a smile, to which the Three assented with hearty amens.

"If I didn't believe in miracles before, I do now." Molly spotted the first stars in the evening sky.

"Wait." Carol leaned forward in her chair. "Is that Hamish walking along the lake? I thought he'd be too tired to move tonight."

But there was no mistaking that tall form, slowly walking toward a nearby bird sanctuary, a dark bulk of binoculars clutched to his chest.

Angus leaped from Molly's lap onto the porch floor. Before she could stop him, the Scottie had dashed down the steps, then toward the lake path.

They all knew calling him would do no good.

Molly, almost too tired to move, made herself stand to track her dog's movements.

A minute later, she was glad she had.

As Angus trotted up to Hamish, their handyman looked first one way, then another, then knelt and petted the Scottie.

What? Molly laid a finger on her lips, then gestured to her friends, who also stood.

Smothering their mirth, they gasped in unison when Hamish pulled something from his pocket, unwrapped it, and gave it to Angus, who snapped it up with gusto.

Hamish had brought a treat for Angus.

"It's—it's a miracle," Molly whispered.

Still stunned, the others nodded.

Just then, the handyman spotted them. "What are you doing out here?" he demanded roughly.

Molly gave him a mischievous grin. "Look out, Hamish! The three Scottish hens are on the loose again. Loch Mallaig will never be the same."

Up to this point, we've been doing all the writing. Now it's *your* turn!

Tell us what you think about this book, the characters, the bad guy, or anything else you'd like to share with us about this series. We can't wait to hear from *you*!

Log on to give us your feedback at:
https://www.surveymonkey.com/r/ScottishBakehouse

Annie's® FICTION